Burnie:
Encouraged to Teach

The Barnabas Chronicles
Book 12

By

Ronna M. Bacon

ISBN 978-1-989699-51-5

Psalm 32:8

I will instruct you and teach you in the way you should go; I will counsel you with my loving eye on you.

Psalm 25:5

Guide me in your truth and tech me, for you are God my Savior, and my hope is in you all day long.

Psalm 143:10

Teach me to do your will, for you are my God; may your good Sprit lead me on level ground.

NKJV

Table of Contents

Chapter 1
Chapter 2
Chapter 3
Chapter 4
Chapter 5
Chapter 6
Chapter 7
Chapter 8
Chapter 9
Chapter 10
Chapter 11
Chapter 12
Chapter 13
Chapter 14
Chapter 15
Chapter 16
Chapter 17
Chapter 18
Chapter 19
Chapter 20
Chapter 21
Chapter 22
Chapter 23
Chapter 24
Chapter 25
Chapter 26
Chapter 27
Chapter 28
Chapter 29
Chapter 30
Chapter 31

Chapter 32
Chapter 33
Chapter 34
Chapter 35
Chapter 36
Chapter 37
Chapter 38
Chapter 39
Chapter 40
Chapter 41
Chapter 42
Chapter 43
Chapter 44
Chapter 45
Chapter 46
Chapter 47
Chapter 48
Chapter 49
Chapter 50
Chapter 51
Chapter 52
Epilogue
Dear Readers

Chapter 1

Staring glumly at his wrist as he tugged against the handcuffs that shackled him to the side rail of the hospital bed, Burnie Cummings wasn't quite sure what had brought him to that or even to the hospital bed in some little town. He stared around the room, his head dropping back on the pillow as his eyes closed. He hurt. All over. And he couldn't remember why. He raised his free hand to stare at the bandages that covered that hand and arm. He had been told, forcefully, that he had burns on them. But no one would tell him how or why. Burnie tugged again at his wrist, desperate to escape yet held in place by two pieces of metal attached by a small chain.

He tried to pray, but he felt that his prayers didn't hit the ceiling. Burnie knew God was there. He just needed some reassurance of that.

Burnie's eyes turned towards the door as it opened and a head appeared, followed by a body and then another man. He frowned.

"Breck? Andy? What are you two doing here?" His voice was low and rough.

"We're here for you." Breck held up a small key. "Dallas gave me this. He's outside, trying to find out why you're chained up." Breck quickly undid the handcuffs and then helped his friend to sit up. "Watch yourself. We were told that you had been unconscious when you were found."

"I was? I don't remember. All I remember is waking up here, with those things on my wrist." Burnie pointed to the handcuffs now laying on the bed. "Can I leave?"

"That's what we're here for." Andy dumped out the plastic bag he had been carrying. "Here. Breck raided your apartment for some clothes."

With Breck's aid, Burnie dressed quickly, his head spinning as he finished. "I don't feel so good, fellows."

"No, we didn't think you would." Breck looked around as the door opened and Dallas, a police detective friend, appeared. "Here's your key. Can we leave?"

"We can. They tried to say that Burnie was a material witness and was on the run from them." Dallas shook his head as he studied his friend, whose dark brown hair was tousled badly and deep green eyes were filled with pain and uncertainty. "Burnie, what did you go and get involved in?"

"If I knew, I wouldn't have." Burnie shoved his feet into his sneakers, staring down at the laces. "I'm not doing those up. They may come and arrest if I take time for that."

Breck grinned for a moment. "Not likely. But let's get you out of here."

The four men moved cautiously away from the hospital, heading for the vehicle that Andy, the Barnabas Foundation pilot, had borrowed from the maintenance man at the small airport. Burnie was tucked into the back seat beside Dallas.

"Burnie, what did you go and do?" Dallas stared at him, unable to see him clearly in the dark.

"I don't know, Dallas. Breck asked me that. I remember leaving on my vacation, needing some time. But I don't remember what happened." Burnie stared out of the window. "I think someone else was there, but I don't know. What happened, anyway?"

"We'll talk, Burnie, once we are into the air. I don't have a good feeling about this small town force." Dallas shifted in his seat to look behind him. "Andy?"

"Five minutes to the airport, Dallas. And then we can take off. I'll just need to do my preflight."

"Okay."

Dallas and Breck hustled Burnie up into the cabin of the Barnabas Foundation plane while Andy did his preflight, buckling him in and then seating themselves. Andy soon was in the cockpit and the plane lifting off.

Once in the air, Breck moved towards Burnie, watching his friend closely, noting the bruises and cuts on his face.

"Burnie, you can't remember anything?"

"About what happened to me?" Burnie shook his head and regretted it, the headache now pounding behind his eyes. "Why'd you make me do that?"

Breck gave a quick grin. "I didn't. You decided to do that." His voice died away as his head tilted. He

—

9

shared a look with Dallas. Both of them had heard something, a soft rustling when there shouldn't have been any.

Breck stood, a finger on his lips to hush Burnie's question. He turned, eyes narrowing, as he moved through the cabin, stopping in front of a cupboard door. It had been closed tightly, he thought, but now was ajar. He yanked at the door, pulling it open quickly, and then reached it, grasping the arm of the youth, as he thought, who was hiding in there, a blanket pulled over themselves.

A startled sob shook the three men as Breck pulled the blanket off the youth.

"What! Wait! You're a lady!" Breck was shocked.

They stared at the young woman who stood in front of them, her hands covering her face as her body shook in fear. Her short auburn curls were tangled and her flannel shirt and jeans were torn, dirty, and covered with burn marks.

"Here! Sit! I'm sorry!" Breck gently shoved her down into a seat, a frown on his face before he reached for her hands, pulling them away from her face.

Startled violet eyes stared at them before she focused on Burnie. She was up from her seat to kneel beside him, a hand reaching to touch his face.

"You're alive. I thought that you were dead!"

"I'm not, but I don't know you. And why are you on this plane?" Burnie's voice sounded harsh and he winced. "I'm sorry. I didn't mean to sound like that.

Here. Sit beside me." He reached for the bottle of water that Dallas held out to him. "Drink this. And then talk."

She swallowed a mouthful too quickly, choking on it, sputtering out water as she coughed.

"I'm sorry. I didn't mean to do that."

"Can you tell us your name?" Burnie's voice had gentled.

"I can. It's Muir Donachie. I'm sorry. I shouldn't have snuck on here. But I heard you talking and that you were looking for someone named Burnie." She turned to Burnie. "Is that you?"

"It is. I'm Burnie. The one who pulled you out of the cupboard is Breck. And this is Dallas." He watched her closely. "Can you tell us why?"

"I guess." She rubbed her hands along her jeans, studying the dirt and debris that covered both her hands and her jeans. "I think I'm responsible for what happened to you."

"You are? And how would that be?"

"You came into the shop that I was working in. Just a little shop where you can buy snacks, soft drinks and some groceries. You heard someone talking to me, took offence at his words and language and removed him. He threatened to come back. You had come back in to talk to me. Then, a fire started in the back of the store and the propane tank exploded. You had made me leave when the fire started. We were running away when the explosion happened. I tried to get back to you, but I couldn't. He was there. He was watching you and then me and threatened you. I couldn't help. I couldn't call for anyone. I had no cell phone, if that's what you call them."

"And then?" Dallas' voice was gentle as he prompted her to continue.

"The police came. I heard them talking to him. He said that you had caused the fire and that they should arrest you. He couldn't prove it. And you weren't awake. I saw them handcuff you and then take you away. They dragged you to one of the cars and just drove away." Her eyes were sorrowful as they watched Burnie.

"Wait a minute! Didn't they call for the paramedics?" Breck shared a look with Dallas, puzzled.

"No, they didn't. We don't have them here, anyway. When they left, he searched for me. I hid. Then I heard the plane and came to the airport, thinking that somehow I could escape. I have never been able to leave this town."

"And then you heard us talking about Burnie?" At her nod, Dallas sat back. "Okay. We'll talk more."

"I don't understand." Muir's eyes searched Dallas' face.

"I'm a police officer, Muir. I can look into this."

Muir looked horrified. "Oh, now! You can't! They'll find my Granny and hurt her. They threatened me with that." The stress that she had been under for an unknown time finally took over her body. Her eyes closed and she was lost to them.

Burnie stared at her. "Is that for real?"

"It's not one of your mystery stories. At least, I don't think it is." Breck commented on Burnie's occupation as a mystery writer. "Dallas, we'll need to look into this."

"And we will. Once we have both Burnie and Muir looked after." Dallas nodded towards Burnie. "We've lost him too."

"So we have." Breck was on his feet. "I need to talk to Andy and then see if I can get through to Barnabas."

Chapter 2

Breck carefully gathered Muir into his arms, heading for the airplane stairs and then his truck, tucking her inside. He turned as he heard Burnie's stumbling steps as he approached, an arm across both Andy's and Dallas' shoulders. They had landed safely on the airstrip on the Barnabas Foundation lands.

"He's alert?" Breck gave a brief grin before concern for his friend coloured his face.

"If you can call it that." Dallas helped Burnie into the truck and then stood back. "What did he get involved in?"

"I have no idea, but I don't like it. I'm glad that you went along."

Dallas nodded. "Will called me. Barnabas had been in touch with him. Did he ever say how he found out about Burnie?"

Breck shook his head. "No. He called as he was heading to a board meeting. Just said that Burnie was in trouble and asked me to fly up with Andy and bring him home. He had asked Will if you would go."

Andy nodded towards the truck. "This is not over for him. At least, I don't think so."

"No, I don't think it is." Breck sighed as he ducked his head to watch Burnie, finding the other man with his arm around Muir, tucking her close to him.

"We're off on another one, fellows. Pray that this time neither one of them is so critically injured."

Doc stood in his apartment doorway twenty minutes later, watching as Breck walked towards him, Muir in his arms, Burnie's stumbling steps leading him that way as well.

"Breck? Who do you have? And what happened to Burnie?"

"This is a stowaway on our plane, Doc. A lady by the name of Muir Donachie. And Burnie was involved in an explosion. We couldn't get a lot of details from his physician. They were very reluctant to talk to us."

"In with you then." Doc peered at the clock. It was getting close to midnight, and he had been up since early morning for his shift at the local Emergency Department. "She can go into that room. Burnie across the hall."

Doc's wife, Anna, gently touched Muir's hair. "What happened to them, Doc? It's not just the explosion for her, is it?"

Doc shook his head. "I don't think so, love. She's too thin." He paused as he lifted the back of her shirt to listen to her chest. "She's been beaten, Anna."

"Oh, Doc! Who would do that?" Anna blinked rapidly. "The poor thing. You finish up and then I'll get her settled. Who was with her?"

"Burnie." Doc was distracted, listening to Muir's heart. "An explosion, the boys said."

"Who?"

"Breck and Dallas." Doc stepped back. "She'll do for the night, love. Get her settled and I'll be back. If she rouses at all, we can talk."

Burnie had dropped back off to sleep, not feeling the sneakers pulled from feet, or the gentle hands as Breck pulled the covers over him. Doc stood for a moment, his eyes on his young friend, even as a prayer was raised for him. Lord, what has he gotten involved in? And is he off on another adventure, just like his friends? If so, please protect him.

Breck stood back beside Doc, uncertainty on his face.

"Doc? He was injured in an explosion a day or so ago. We tried to get information on him but the hospital refused. He was also handcuffed to his bed."

"Handcuffed? That's not our Burnie. Has he said much?" Doc peered at Breck and then down at Burnie.

"Not really. Muir did mention that he was unconscious, or dead as she thought." Breck looked behind him. "She's worried about her grandmother. She doesn't want us talking to anyone."

"And that won't happen, you not talking to anyone, not if I know you fellows. You'll be deep into an investigation on the morrow." Doc walked towards Burnie, bending over him. "Did he say why the bandage?"

"He said burns, but I really question that, Doc." Breck was hesitant to say what he really thought. Lord, please heal our friend.

Doc reached to unwrap the bandage, a puzzled look on his face. "What are they talking about? There are no burns."

Breck shared a look with Doc and then reached for the bandage, feeling it. "There's something in here, Doc. Something small and metal?"

"Then I suggest that you remove it from here." Doc peered at the clock. "It's not too late. Take it into town and give it to the police. Dallas can get it from them."

"I agree. I'll check in on him in the morning, Doc." Breck walked away, leaving Doc to assess Burnie.

Rousing in the early morning hours, Burnie lifted his head and frowned. This wasn't his apartment. Where was he? He slipped from his bed, stumbling over his feet and the blankets, before he felt his way to the door. Cracking it open, he watched as a lady walked the halls, her arms wrapped around herself, muttering quietly. He opened his door fully, startling her.

"I'm sorry!" Burnie's words were barely audible. "I didn't mean to scare you." He looked around her, seeing Anna in their own bedroom doorway. "Can't sleep?"

Muir stared at him, her violet eye huge. "No. I don't know where I am. Is he here?"

Burnie cautiously reached out a hand, finding hers reaching for his. "No, I don't think so. I'm not sure who you mean." He led her to the kitchen, seating her and then switching on the light over the sink. Anna had followed, standing back from the door where she could watch Muir. "What would you like to drink?"

"Water, I guess." Muir rubbed her hands on her legs. "I don't want to make any work."

"You're not. I'm making coffee. Anna had all sorts of different teas or hot chocolate." Muir's mouth dropped open when Burnie opened that cupboard door.

"I didn't think they made that many." She was on her feet, leaning against him as she counted them. "There are so many."

"Pick one. It won't matter to Anna."

Muir reached for one that said peppermint. "I have always wanted to know what peppermint tea tasted like. We could only get tea once in a while. Granny and I didn't have a lot of money."

"Then, peppermint tea it is." Burnie didn't move, his eyes on her as she continued to lean against him, staring at the selection of teas and coffee. "Muir, are you hungry?"

Her eyes turned to him again, even as she frowned before she saw the time. "Burnie? It four in the morning. It's not breakfast time."

"Doesn't matter. Anna and Doc won't care. Doc is sometimes up at this time of the morning. He's a doctor and works in an Emergency room."

"He is? He does? Oh, that's what I always wanted to do. But I couldn't afford to go to school." Muir turned, stopping abruptly as she saw Anna standing inside the kitchen door. "I'm sorry. I am

—

18

disturbing you. I shouldn't have." She looked down at her nightwear and the dressing gown that she have found to wear. "If you tell me where my clothes are, I'll get dressed and leave. Only I don't know where I am." Distress coloured her voice.

Anna simply reached to hug the younger woman, finding her stiffen at first and then reach to hug her back, even as sobs shook Muir's body. Burnie stood, his eyes on Muir, not knowing that his heart that she had already staked a claim on was visible in his eyes.

Chapter 3

Burnie paced his office later that morning. He needed to work, he could feel the plot and characters in his latest novel burning inside him, but his thoughts were on Muir. After he had fed her toast and tea, she had barely been able to keep her eyes open and had shuffled off back to her rest. Anna had watched her before she simply hugged Burnie, a prayer for the young couple whispered in his ear.

He finally dropped to his chair, booting up his computer and then staring at the screen. He sighed, reaching instead for his Bible, needing that time with his Father. An hour later, he set it aside and rose, heading back for Doc's. He paused as he entered the lobby, watching Muir as she just stood and then turned in a circle.

Burnie smiled as he approached her, standing just short of where she was, waiting for her to turn back towards him as she spun. Muir stopped abruptly as she saw him.

"This place is so big!" Her eyes were huge as she spoke.

"It is." He grinned at her, reaching out a hand and then leading her to one of the two seating areas in the lobby. "It's our home, Muir. You met Breck last night. He has an apartment here as do I. On the main floor are the offices that each of us fellows have. And

---

then we each have an apartment here on the three floors."

"You do? They must be small."

"Muir, you saw Doc and Anna's place?" He waited patiently until she nodded. "All of our apartments are that big. And there are some that are used for visitors or for short-time occupancy. And before you ask, there are fourteen of us fellows. Eleven are married. One couple has a set of twins and I know two more who will adding to their family in the next few months."

"There are? How tall is this place, anyway?" Muir craned her neck, trying to guess the height. She stared at the skylights. "Those are pretty. I would not have thought of having stained glass up there."

"Barnabas' mother wanted that. The stained glass is sandwiched between panes of glass that are almost unbreakable."

"They are? Someone went to a lot of work." She was on her feet, moving away from him and towards the door. "Are the doors locked?"

"Not during the day." He ran after her, reaching for her hand, waiting for her to pull away, surprised when she didn't. "We can go outside and walk around the gardens if you like."

"We can? We're allowed?" Muir stared at him. "No one will say anything? I'm not used to that."

"We can and we are allowed. No, no one will say anything, unless you are in danger. The grounds

—

are our home as well. Come on. The roses are still in bloom."

Burnie watched as Muir slowly walked the rose garden, his steps matching hers. She reached to touch a petal on one.

"These are so beautiful. Granny had one, but it really didn't grow much. She was always so disappointed in it." Muir breathed in the scent from the roses. "There are just so many colours. I am not sure which one I like best."

Burnie smiled before he reached for his pocket knife, finding the blooms that were just opening, and picking a selection for her. His knife made short work of the thorns before he turned, finding shock on her face.

"Burnie! You shouldn't have done that! We're not allowed!"

Burnie simply wrapped her into a hug, the roses resting against her back. "Muir, I don't understand why you're stating these things, but here? We're allowed to come outside or stay inside. We can roam wherever we want on the lands. We can pick whatever flowers we want. There is also a vegetable garden that we all work in and can pick what we want from there. The fruit trees? We can pick the fruit."

She finally nodded against him. "Okay. I wasn't allowed to do that. Do you have any animals?"

Burnie grinned. "Other than a couple of kittens, cats, and two dogs? No."

"I had to look after the chickens for the store owner. I won't miss them." Muir moved back, her eyes on him. "Burnie?"

"Here." He held up the bouquet of roses. "There's are for you. Roses for a beautiful lady."

"Oh, you don't mean me. I'm not beautiful. I'm ugly and a runt." Muir was just above average height for a lady and had the classical looks of a beautiful lady who would age well.

Chapter 4

Standing where he could watch Muir, Barnabas caught the look on Burnie's face and sighed. *Here we go again, don't we, Lord? Another adventure? I don't know how much more our fellows can take, that's the thing. It just keeps adding on to our stress. But You are in control. That much I know.*

Burnie looked up and around as he felt eyes on them, a frown on his face. He nodded towards Barnabas before he looked behind him. Someone else was there. He just wasn't sure who.

Burnie reached for Muir's hand, turning her towards the main walkway, pausing as he felt her steps slowing. He searched her face, seeing the momentary fear and the puzzlement on her face.

"Muir, this is Barnabas. He's my boss, and he is also represents the Barnabas Foundation." Burnie waited, not finding her responding. "It's okay, Muir. You're welcome here. In fact, Barnabas is the one who sent Breck, Dallas, and Andy to find me yesterday."

"He did? Why?" Muir didn't take her eyes from Barnabas.

"Because he's a friend. He does that." Burnie nudged her closer. "He won't bite, Muir. Nor will he harm you."

"He won't? I don't know him."

Barnabas grinned, lighting up his face. "No, you don't, and you are correct to be careful. But I am a friend of Burnie's, and I hope to be your friend. I found out yesterday that Burnie needed me. I just did what I do best, sent in help."

"Oh! I'm not used to that." Muir's hand tightened on Burnie's. "Burnie? What happened?"

"I don't know, Muir. The store exploded and burnt. So did my car." Burnie watched in horror as her face crumpled.

"It's my fault. I did that."

Burnie gave a growl of disbelief and simply swept an arm around her. "No, you didn't. Whoever set the fire did that. It's not your fault." He exchanged a glance with Barnabas. "Is that what you have been living with?"

Muir finally nodded. "It's always my fault. That's what he told me. He would beat me if I didn't say that."

Burnie froze, his words dying on his lips, as he stared down at the head resting against his shoulder. He shared another look of concern with Barnabas.

"He told you that? He beat you?" At her nod, Burnie grew angry. "Who told you that?"

"The owner of the store. It was the only work I could find in our village. He threatened Granny if I didn't do what he said. I was finally able to get Granny away from him. That's when he beat me the worst. He would beat me to try and find out where she was. I couldn't tell him." Muir's head went back as she looked up at Burnie. "I miss her. And you're tall!"

"I am, Muir." Burnie gave a grin that didn't reach his eyes. "Would you like your Granny to come here?"

She nodded and then sighed. "But I can't. I don't have anywhere to live."

Barnabas's hand rested on her back, startling her. "Muir, you have a home. You have a home here for as long as you want it. Anna will welcome you to stay with them. There is also an apartment available right beside Burnie. It's furnished and everything. You can use it."

"I can? Oh, that would be wonderful. But I don't have any work. I can't pay you."

"Muir, we don't expect you to pay. No one who has a need is ever turned away." Barnabas was patient as he watched the conflicting emotions cross her face. "We don't charge people who are in need. It's part of how we encourage one another."

Muir finally nodded, her eyes on her roses. The effect of being free from the cruel store owner and his physical and verbal abuse was hard for her to understand. To have a male reach out to her in this way? She just didn't understand it.

"I'm sorry. Burnie picked these for me." She tried to shove the roses at Barnabas, who simply grinned and shook his head.

"No, keep them. Beautiful roses for a beautiful lady. That's what they're for, Muir. All the ladies pick the flowers." Barnabas pointed towards the building. "How be we go back in? I can walk you through the apartment next to Burnie. And then we can talk about your grandmother coming to live with you."

"Thank you." Muir blinked back the tears that clouded her eyes. "No one has ever been so kind."

"This is just the start, Muir. Once you have met the fellows and their ladies, I assure you that you will find everyone kind here.

"I will?" Muir turned to Burnie, finding him nodding in agreement.

Chapter 5

Walking through the apartment next to Burnie that night, Muir wrapped her arms around herself. She didn't think that she had seen such a beautiful home. And to know that it was hers? And her Granny's? She felt like she was in heaven. It would take a while for the fear that gripped her in such a tight grasp to fade, but Burnie had sensed that she was fighting to free herself. He had simply hugged her, kissed her cheek and stepped back as Anna had approached her.

Muir spun and almost ran for the master bedroom, sliding to a stop to stare around at the soft yellow and cream walls and trim, feeling for the first time, she thought, a sense of peace and hope. Burnie had done that, she thought. If he had not been there, she would not have been able to escape. She was afraid to talk to him, to tell him what she had overheard. She had prayed for someone to walk in and rescue her and Burnie had.

Approaching the bed, Muir stared down at the piles of clothing, all brand new, that Anna and she thought the lady's name was Cadee had brought in for her. She couldn't remember the last time that she had had new clothes. Certainly not is such an abundance. She had tried to protest but Cadee had simply shrugged, hugged her, and told her to enjoy them.

Muir stopped finally in the kitchen, her hair wrapped in a towel that she kept fingering, her eyes searching the kitchen. She touched the different appliances and then investigated the cupboards, finding more small appliances and an abundance of food stuffs. She didn't realize that Cadee had gone to the other ladies and together they had shopped for her.

Sinking to the floor, Muir wept. God, I think that You heard my complaints and just dropped me down into heaven. She finally crept to her bed and slept, wishing that her Granny was there with her, but knowing that she couldn't be. She didn't know that Burnie had gone to Breck, handing him her grandmother's name and where she was. Burnie had managed to find that out without Muir understanding what he was asking or why.

Breck had frowned for a moment before his face cleared.

"We'll bring her here, Burnie. Muir needs her. She hasn't said anything about her parents?"

"Not a word. She's so overwhelmed right now." Burnie paused, blinking back tears as he thought of Muir that day. "She was beaten, Breck. She has so little self-esteem right now."

"I know she does. Barnabas spoke with me." Breck sat back in his armchair, reaching for the ever-present pad of paper and pen. "What do we do for her?"

"Cadee took care of clothes for her. The ladies stocked her kitchen, although I'm not sure how well she'll cope with the modern appliances." Burnie bit at his lip. "We need to find something for her to do, something that will build her up. I hate that she's so downtrodden."

"We'll get there, Burnie. Right now, the best thing is for her to rest. She's been through a harrowing experience from what I understand. I know you have deadlines for your book."

"I do, but I can work at anytime, most days. Do you know she asked if we could go outside? If we were allowed?"

Breck sat forward. "She said that? It sounds as if she was kept a prisoner."

"That's what I think. I have remembered the words directed at her." Burnie paused, a sick feeling in his stomach. "There was a reason for how she was treated."

"Human trafficking?" Breck was quick to pick up on Burnie's thought.

"I think so. I think he was threatening her grandmother to shape her into doing what he wanted. It almost succeeded."

"It has. Did Doc talk to you?"

"He did. He's puzzled as to why they told me I had a burn, other than to put the GPS tracker on me. Thanks for looking after that." Burnie paused. "He won't say, but I know that Muir was beaten."

"More than once, I would suspect." Breck sat back, a prayer in his heart. "Burnie, you don't have to answer, but I know your heart. How invested are you in Muir already?"

Burnie didn't answer right away, knowing that was something he had to pray through. He finally looked up at Breck, finding his friend watching him closely.

"At the moment, I know I am attracted to her. She is a beautiful lady who I want to get to know. But I have to be careful of her. I can't rush her into anything."

"No, you can't. It's different for her. She watches to see who is going to hurt her. Only prayer can help to change that. If I might suggest, talk to Buckley. See if Locklin will speak with her. That might help."

"I will. Buckley and Locklin are away for a couple of days. I'll call when he's back." Burnie finally stood, stopping his walk towards the door as Breck's hand came down on his shoulder.

"Let me pray with you, Burnie, before you leave. You're carrying a burden tonight, my friend.

Chapter 6

Two days later, Muir wandered the lobby of the building, not seeing how intently that she was being watched by Breck. He stood just out of her line of sight, praying for her, not quite sure how to do that. She had not told Burnie much more than she already had. The fellows were concerned, working away as they could with the little information that Burnie had been able or willing to give them.

Muir paused in front of the lobby door before she pushed it open and stepped outside in a hesitant manner. She wasn't used to that kind of freedom, not any more. The store owner who had employed her had made sure that she knew she was not allowed outside unless he told her that she could. She had been like that for months, she thought. Lord, I'm trying. But it's hard to let go.

Moving around the building, Muir found her way to the rose garden, a garden that she just knew she would spend a lot of time in. She hesitated as a dog approached her, sitting in front of her, a paw raised for her to shake. Jumping as she heard a male laugh from in front of her, her eyes shot towards him in a frightened manner.

"It's okay. This is Kade. He's friendly. I'm Bradon. I live here as well." Bradon waited, having heard of Muir from his wife, Ennis. "You must be Muir, Burnie's friend."

"I'm Muir, but I'm not sure if I'm Burnie's friend or not. I caused him a lot of problems."

"Not from what he says." Bradon pointed to a bench nearby. "Would you like to sit? Kade, move out of the way."

Muir studied him for a moment before she nodded, sitting on the edge of the bench. "This is nice here."

"It is. Except for Barnabas and Breck, we're all from different provinces. This is home now and has been for a number of years. Those of us who are married? Most of our wives are from the area." Bradon watched Muir closely, seeing her begin to relax a little. "Where's Burnie?"

Muir frowned at him. "I have no idea. I have not seen him at all today. He brings me here and then abandons me." Sighing to herself, she apologized. "I'm sorry. I didn't mean that. I know he's writing and has to. I am just thankful that he came and that I could get away. I don't think I would have lasted there much longer."

"What do you mean?"

Shrugging, Muir didn't respond, her eyes on the ants scurrying around her toes. "I heard him talking." Her voice was barely a whisper. "He was planning on sending me somewhere. I didn't like what I was hearing him say about me." She looked up, bewilderment and pain in her eyes. "I am glad that I am not there, but I think I brought danger to here."

Bradon gave a soft laugh, even as he noted Burnie heading their way. "Muir, you have no idea what we have been through here. Some of us almost died. I was drowned and revived. My wife, Ennis, was stabbed. Just a bit ago, Locklin, Buckley's wife, was given an overdose and her heart stopped. So no, you're not bringing anything that we haven't dealt with."

Muir stared at him, her mouth slightly open before she shook her head. "That's hard to believe. Anna talked to me, told me about all of you but she never told me that." She jumped as Burnie's arm came around her.

"It's true, Muir. And we all want to help you stop this man from hurting you or anyone else." Burnie kept his eyes on her profile.

"You do?" Muir kept her eyes on Bradon. "All of you?"

"All of us, Muir. We would like to consider you a friend, if we may." Bradon smiled even as Kade stood up at Muir's knee, sniffing at her face.

Muir's arms went around the dog as she hugged him, a swipe of Kade's tongue against her face.

"He's beautiful. I always wanted a dog, but we just couldn't do it. Granny only had a small pension that we had to live on. I tried to find work but it was hard." She sniffed, not willing to give into her tears.

"You don't have to worry about that here, Muir. If you want a dog, or a cat, or even a bird, you can have that." Burnie watched as she mulled over his words and then turned to him.

"I can? Oh, I have so wanted a cat. We had a kitten when I was just so tiny but it disappeared."

"Then, that's what we can do today. I know of someone who has some kittens that they want to re-home." Burnie waited for her to speak, his eyes meeting Bradon's and finding only concern in them.

"I don't think so, Burnie. I need to find work first." Muir was on her feet, running for the building, not hearing Burnie's call for her to wait.

"Burnie? What just happened?" Bradon was on his feet, standing beside Burnie.

"I'm not sure, Bradon. I am really not sure." Burnie sighed. "This is so hard. I don't know how to approach her or what to say. She's terrified, I know that."

"Her grandmother?"

Burnie nodded. "I suspect so. Branigan and Brady are heading out with Dallas to bring her here. They leave early in the morning. It's really not that far from here."

"Will it help her?" Bradon paced beside Burnie as he walked slowly back towards the building.

"I pray it does. She is so scared for her grandmother. If we can get the two of them together, maybe Muir will open up more."

Chapter 7

Seeking refuge and solace in the rose garden late the next afternoon, Muir reached to touch a red and white rose. She sighed. Granny, I want to see you, but I am afraid to see you. He'll find me and then you. I just wish, God, that I had never been born. She turned as she heard a soft sound, blinking rapidly, before she was running towards the tall, slender, older lady who stood watching her, arms open to receive her.

Barnabas stood and watched from the distance, Burnie beside him.

"Was there any trouble, Barnabas?"

"No, Brady said there wasn't. Her grandmother stood for a moment assessing them, asked what took them so long, and just reached for a bag sitting on the table in the apartment hallway. She told them that God had spoken to her, that she was to expect three men that very day, and that they would take her to her granddaughter. She also stated that she had been given their names."

Burnie shot a glance at Barnabas before he nodded. "Yes, in this situation, God would do just that, wouldn't he?"

"He would. Come find me later, Burnie. We need to talk." Barnabas walked away, his heart raised in prayer for his friend and his lady and her Granny as she called her.

—

Moira Donachie finally stood back, her hands on her granddaughter's upper arms and studied her. She's thin, Lord, thinner than I ever remember seeing her. What did that monster do to her? Please, Lord, we need healing, the pair of us.

Muir wiped at her eyes, a smile finally reaching them. "Granny? How? I didn't think that we should be in touch."

"God willed otherwise, love. He brought three young men to my door earlier today and had already told me their names and that I was to go with them. That they would bring me to you. That you were safe." Moira turned Muir back towards the building, their arms around one another. "You have a beautiful place to live, Muir."

"For us, Granny. For us. Barnabas told me that the home here is for us."

"He did, did he? Then I guess it is." Moira watched Burnie as he stood, roses in his hands for them, and just waited. "This young man in front of us?"

"Burnie? He was hurt, Granny, when the store exploded. He and his friends brought me here." Moira gave a wavering smile at Burnie. "He's been wonderful and kind, Granny."

"Like the knights of old that I wove into your bedtime stories?" At Muir's nod, Granny smiled. "Then, Muir, why the hesitation that I hear in your voice?"

"I'm afraid, Granny, that the monster from home will find me. He threatened horrible things. I don't even want to tell you about them. He told me that if I showed any interest in anyone, he would kill that man."

"Somehow, love, I don't think that this Burnie will let him. I hear there are a number of men who live here who have had adventures. His friends talked today, I think in part, to reassure me that we would be safe." Moira stopped them in front of Burnie. "We will talk, love, alone and then with this man of yours."

Burnie's smile lit up his face. "Flowers for two beautiful ladies." He then stepped around them, moving between them, and holding out his arms. "May I escort you to the meal that I know Anna has prepared for us? Tomorrow, it is our usual potluck meal in the building. Tonight, we'll go easy on you."

"You will, will you, young man?" Moira gave a soft laugh. "I like you. You'll be good for my Muir."

Muir stared at her grandmother, aghast that she had said that. Moira just shook her head at her granddaughter. She and her Lord had had plenty of time to talk, she thought. Muir needs someone just like Burnie. He'll draw her out, teach her how to live. She needs that. That monster beat her down. Now, to settle with him.

Late that night, Moira stood watching her granddaughter sleep, sorrow on her face, a prayer in her heart. Lord, protect my girl. I know that she's not safe. Not yet. I know what that man was. I hated for her to go and work for him, but there was not a lot of work in our community. And we were prevented from leaving. How Muir managed to get me out, I don't know. But she did, and because she did, You were able to get her out. Thank you, Dear Lord. Moira then turned and sought her own rest, a peace in her heart for her beloved granddaughter.

Burnie stood on the balcony outside his living room doorway, his head tilted back to watch the clouds scudding across the night sky. It was a favourite time of day for him, one where he could commune with his Lord. Tonight, his heart was full of thankfulness that Muir and Moira were together again. He had spoken briefly with Moira, heard her story in part, and then had just hugged her. He had never known his grandparents. Or his parents for that matter. He had been placed in foster care as an infant, and no one had ever offered to adopt him. That had always puzzled him and driven him to stay apart from people. The men and ladies in the building had changed that. He had become part of a large family, he thought, when Barnabas had tracked him down and offered him a position with the Barnabas Foundation. Barnabas had simply waved away Burnie's protests that he couldn't, that Burnie wanted to be a writer, stating that part of the mandate of the Foundation was to encourage others, and this was what Burnie needed.

Chapter 8

The next evening, chatter and laughter filled the conference room that was used for the monthly potluck dinners the Foundation family had. Moira, welcomed by all of them, stood beside Anna, watching them all but in particular her Muir as she stood as close to Burnie as she could get, her hand tight in his.

"Anna? This is a wonderful family that my Muir has dropped into."

"And you as well, Moira. They are a good bunch. Brady said that they explained what had happened to them all."

"That he did. God protected them, didn't he? He protected my Muir and brought that young Burnie into her life just as she needed him."

"He did that." Anna exchanged a look with Blair and Breck who stood beside Anna.

"I fear for her, though. The man she worked for will not let her go. A number of young ladies disappeared from our village and those who came through were at risk."

Breck rubbed his hand along the back of his neck. "Moira? Are you suggesting that he removed them?"

"I can do more than that, young man. I have proof that I have worked on over the last few years that I can turn over to you. I feared that Muir would disappear into that world and I would never see her again."

"She's here, now. We will do our best to protect her." Breck hesitated as Moira shook her head. "There's a problem?"

"There is. He is a very vindictive man. With Muir escaping him? He will come after her. You fellows that were with her? He'll come after you. But he'll go after Burnie in particular. This man seeks revenge and violence against those who thwart him." Moira studied her granddaughter as she moved away hesitantly with Cadee and Ennis. "She's scared, Breck. More scared that she will admit to anyone."

"She is. We've seen that." Breck sighed. "Did you know that he had beaten her?"

"I suspected as much. I felt her flinch when I hugged her yesterday. That is not my Muir. She was always free with her hugs."

Burnie had moved to stand near them. "Moira? I think you and I need to have a talk, in private, but I will state this here and now. I will do my utmost to protect our Muir."

"Our Muir, is it, young Burnie? Then, we will work together, you and I, and your friends as well. Now, I see that Barnabas is trying to get our attention. What do we do now?"

Muir turned as she felt someone beside her, watching Burnie as he stood there, his head bowed as Buckley blessed their meal. She was distracted, she thought, as he reached for her hand, his grasp tight and

---

warm and comforting. She looked up as the prayer finished, to find his eyes on her, a light in them that she didn't or wouldn't allow herself to understand.

Fynn watched the pair closely before she turned to Brady.

"He's serious about her, isn't he?"

Brady studied his friend. "I would think so. He's like us. One look and he knows." He gave her a quick kiss. "We have to pray for them."

"We are. The ladies are meeting on Monday, seeing as tomorrow is Sunday. I would like to ask Muir and her grandmother to join us."

"Ask, but don't worry if they say no. Muir needs healing, Fynn, in so many ways."

"She does. She's like a lost little kitten. Burnie will bring her out."

"That he will." Brady turned away at a question from Branigan, leaving Fynn to watch Muir closely.

Muir stood at the end of the evening, feeling overwhelmed and lost, not quite sure how she would fit in, if she ever would. Berneen and Devaney had approached her, quick smiles on their faces.

"Muir? The ladies in the building are meeting on Monday for a Bible study. We're all off during the day for a change. We would like you and your Grandmother to join us, if you wish." Berneen didn't push, knowing that she couldn't.

"A Bible study? Oh, I don't know. Can I let you know?"

"You can do just that." Devaney spoke up. "We're in the apartment next to you. We're meeting at 9, so come if you wish. If you don't, that's okay. We understand. We've all been the new kids here at one time or another."

Muir nodded, her eyes searching the room for all the ladies. "I understand that. It's just that you wouldn't know that."

"We were. And we would really like you to come, but if you're not able to, maybe next time."

The ladies spoke for a bit longer before the two walked away.

"She's so scared, Berneen."

"I know. I haven't heard what all happened to her. But we can still pray for her."

Cadee had approached them, overhearing their conversation. "Muir reminds me of some of the young girls that come through the shelter, who had been abused and threatened. Some have escaped from human traffickers."

"You don't think?" Berneen drew in her breath. "Until she tells us, we don't speculate. We pray."

"That we do." Cadee looked contrite. "I didn't mean to insinuate that was what had happened to Muir."

"No, you weren't. But something did." Devaney shot a look behind her. "Good, Burnie's with her. He'll take care of her."

"He will. He's needed that special lady. Muir is it."

Chapter 9

Staring at the gates that led to the Barnabas Foundation property, the man hammered at the steering wheel in the battered truck that he drove. He glared at the woods surrounding the gates, knowing that he wouldn't make his way through there. She was there, he thought, and I need to get to her but I can't. Not yet. I need to find someone familiar with the property who can help.

Shoving the truck transmission into gear, he gunned the motor, speeding off, gravel flying behind him as he did so. Brandon and Brendon exchanged a glance as they stopped at the gate before following him.

"What's his problem?" Brandon shot a look behind him before he turned back around, his hands steady on the wheel.

Brendon shrugged, his eyes on the photo that he had snapped. "Good. I was able to get the plate number. Now, to send it on to Dallas." He looked up and through the windshield. "You don't suppose that it's the man from up north?"

"More than likely. He'll have had some way of tracking us." Brandon pulled off into a coffee shop. "This is where you were to meet?"

"It is. Thanks, Brandon. Four work for you?"

"It does. I'll see you then. Listen, if you hear from Dallas, let me know. But we need to let Burnie know."

"On it. I sent him a text with the picture as well. He's deep into something, he said, and would get back to me."

"His books! See you tonight."

Brendon watched Brandon drive away before he pulled out his phone again. Dallas had been in touch.

"Dallas?"

"Brendon? Where was this taken?" Dallas sounded distracted.

"Just outside the gates. He had been parked on the side of the road and pulled out in front of us. Why?"

"Where's Burnie?"

"Still at the building. He said he had to concentrate on some stuff for his publisher today, proofreading or something like that."

"He'll have to talk to me. I'm heading that way. Is Muir there?"

"I would suspect so. The ladies are getting together for a Bible study today and asked Muir and Moira to join them. They hadn't said that they would, though."

"Okay. Stay safe, my friend. If this man knows you snapped a picture of his vehicle, you're not safe."

Brendon grew still. "He's that bad?"

"He is. He's all and more than what both Muir and Moira think. We need to watch them closely. He'll go after Burnie just for getting Muir away from him." Dallas was gone before Brendon could say another word.

A quick text to both Brandon and Barnabas and then Brendon was running to meet his friend. They were off on a quick road trip that day but Brendon's heart was raised in prayer for his friends.

Burnie gave a groan as he heard a knock at his office door, glancing down at the paperwork he was almost through, before he rose and headed for the door, opening to find Dallas standing there.

"Dallas? You're here? Come on in. I've about ten minutes left on paperwork that I have to get done and in this morning. I think the coffee is still okay." Burnie was back at his desk, immersed in his documents, not noticing that Dallas had made a fresh pot of coffee and set a new mug down beside him.

Finally sitting back, his documents done and sent on to his publisher, Burnie reached for the mug of coffee and sipped.

"You made fresh?"

"I did. That sludge that was there had to have been from first thing this morning." Dallas simply grinned at his friend. "How are you faring, Burnie?"

Burnie shrugged. "To tell you the truth? I feel like I just jumped off a cliff into an undertow,"

"Good analogy. I think that's exactly what you've done." Dallas pulled out his phone. "Did you get a text from Brendon?"

"I think so." Burnie reached for his phone, paling as he read it. "I hadn't read it before. He was outside the gates?"

"He was. He took off when Brandon drove through them. What we need to determine is if this is the man from up north. Where's Muir?"

"With her grandmother." Burnie squinted at the clock. "They might be with the ladies. I'm not sure. Their Bible study is likely over by now." He was on his feet, heading for the door when Dallas' voice stopped him.

"Burnie?" When Burnie turned back, Dallas stared hard at him. "Think hard about what you are going to say and do. She's not used to the world. She's been sheltered up there. To have had to work for this storekeeper and be abused like she has been? She needs tenderness."

"I know, Dallas, but she's also got a tough streak in her. I've seen it." Burnie waited for Dallas to exit before he locked his office door and headed for the stairs.

Chapter 10

Standing in the lobby, Burnie watched as Muir and Moira walked towards the elevators, not seeing the two men waiting for them. He shook his head. He needed to talk with her, he supposed, and warn her that she needed to be aware of her surroundings.

Muir looked up, sensing eyes on her, frowning first at Dallas and then smiling at Burnie. Moira reached to hug Burnie and then hugged Dallas, surprising him.

"Ladies? Having a good morning?" Burnie just grinned at the frown Muir directed his way.

"We were. We spent the morning in the garden. I'm sorry. I just couldn't face all the ladies this morning." Muir looked upset at that.

"They understand, Muir." Burnie reached to hug her. "God was there with you, wasn't He?"

"He was." Muir's face lit up, showing the beauty that was there. "But you're here? I thought you had to work."

"I'm finished what I needed to do for my publisher. The plot of my next book is still mulling around in my mind. My characters aren't sharing what they want to do, so I have to wait. Listen, Muir, Moira? Can we talk?"

"We can, boys, but it's lunchtime. We'll eat first, spend some time in prayer and then talk. Dallas? You have time?"

"I do, Moira. I do. I have some interviews to do but that's later this afternoon. And I'm not on call, so I can take some time." Dallas walked off with her, climbing the steps beside her.

Muir watched her grandmother closely before she spoke.

"Burnie? What happened?"

"Your storekeeper? What kind of vehicle did he drive?"

"A brand new truck. I don't know the make. He used to have a beaten up one but that one he burnt."

"He did?" Burnie paused, then pulled out his phone. "This truck was outside of the gates this morning. Brendon snapped a photo of it."

Muir leaned against him, her hand tilting his in order to see the photo. "That's his brother's truck. They have tracked me down?"

"I would assume so. Dallas would have had to say what force he worked for." Burnie's arm came around her as they walked up the stairs. "That's what he needs to talk to you about."

"All I can say is that his brother is as brutal as he is. There have always been rumours about what they are involved in. Any female in the area avoided them as much as they could." Her frown deepened. "Is he that desperate to get me back in his control?"

"I would think so, Muir."

Late that afternoon, Moira found her granddaughter stretched out on the couch in their apartment, sound asleep. She reached for a blanket to cover her, a hand resting on her head as she prayed for Muir. She turned as she heard a tap at the door and opened it to find Burnie, Breck, and Barnabas there.

"Gentlemen? Come in. The kitchen, I think. Muir is asleep."

"She is?" Barnabas frowned for a moment. "We needed to speak with her."

"First, we pray. Then, we talk. And then I'll awaken her. She's rundown physically, boys, as well as emotionally and mentally. She needs time to heal."

"Unfortunately, Moira, it doesn't look as if that will happen." Breck slid a photo across the table to her. "This man was around this morning. Muir told Burnie that he's the storekeeper's brother."

"He is." Moira paused, before she shook her head. "He's been after Muir for years. I have been so afraid that he would harm her."

"But he hasn't, yet. We plan to see that doesn't happen." Breck's voice was stern and his eyes raised to where Muir stood in the doorway. "Muir? I thought your grandmother said that you were asleep."

"I was, but I'm not. What is this about Walter?"

Burnie reached to pull her down beside him, keeping his arm across the back of her chair, just touching her. "We talked, Muir. He's in the area."

"I know he is. But why?"

"He's looking for you, Muir." Barnabas caught the look that the two ladies shared. "Why?"

"Why? It's obvious. Stewart didn't like that I left." Muir rubbed at her forehead, a headache starting. "I can't do this." She was on her feet, running from them, the apartment door slamming behind her.

Burnie gave a sound and then was on his feet, following her, catching her in the lobby and just holding her, not seeing Baird and Berneen and Blair and Devaney as they were heading out. His audible prayer finally reached through her panic and she relaxed against him.

"Muir? How do we do this? How do we keep you safe?"

Muir shrugged, her hair brushing against his chin. "I don't know, Burnie. I don't know. How do we? And why would you care?"

"Why would I care?" Burnie's arms tightened around her. "I care about you, Muir, not just as a friend, but as a beautiful lady who I would like to get to know better. God brought us together, Muir."

"He did?" She leaned back enough to look up at him, seeing the look in his eye. "Just what are you saying, Burnie?"

"That I would like to date you, be your beau, look to the future." He watched with compassion as her eyes closed and a single tear traced down her cheek.

"Do you mean that? Burnie, do you really mean that?" Muir looked back up at him. "Do you know how I prayed for someone to walk in and save me? And then you did?"

Chapter 11

Burnie directed them to a seat in one of the lobby sitting areas, his eyes on Brennen as he and Buckley were seated on the other side, a nod towards them. He seated Muir, his arm still around her.

"I mean that, Muir. At first, it was because you were a lady in distress. That's when I stepped in, to protect you at the store. Now? I'm starting to understand who you are and who you can be. That's my prayer, sweetheart, that God will work in your life and bring out the beauty that's there."

Muir listened to him pray, before she looked up at him. "But it's dangerous. He's an evil man with a huge streak of meanness and anger in him."

"He's a coward and bully. We'll take him on, you and I, and Granny, and all my friends here. He will not win. He will not overcome. We may have to go through things, but we'll emerge victorious."

"You sound so sure." Muir was hesitant, knowing the character of the man who Burnie was willing to take on for her.

"I am. I have no doubt that he and his henchmen will try their best to overcome us and take you back. We won't let them." Burnie hugged her tighter. "I promise that I will do my best to protect you and Granny."

"That's my fear, Burnie. Granny."

"We'll look after her. She's a smart lady, your Granny is. I imagine right now that she, Breck, and Barnabas are coming up with a plan. I'm not sure that we'll like it."

Muir found that hilarious. Her charming bell-like laughter echoed through the lobby. "You can count on that, Burnie. Granny can come up with some wild plans. She used to do that with my bed-time stories. Now, about Walter?"

"Dallas called before we came up to find you. Walter was arrested on a break-and-enter charge in town. When they looked into his record, he's wanted for so many charges and violations of his parole that he will be going back to prison and that will be today. So for now, he's out of the picture."

"And Stewart will be angrier at me. I know that. He'll come after you." Muir chewed at her lower lip.

"He can come and try. He will not succeed. Not in the long run." Burnie sat, Muir cuddled against him, trying to come up with words that would calm and reassure her both.

"Burnie? What was in the store that he didn't want anyone to find?" Muir's question got Burnie off guard.

"You think that there was something there?"

Muir nodded. "I do. I think that he had someone hidden there. I would hear sounds in the night, like someone walking around."

Burnie paled. "Are you saying what I think you are? That he killed someone?"

———

"I am. It was always rumoured that he had killed before. How do we prove it?"

"I'll talk to Dallas, see what he or Will Peters, the police chief, can do. It may mean that the provincial force can move in and do an investigation. We'll have to see. Did you have a mayor?"

"Yeah, Walter."

"Oh, I see. But if Walter's not able to act, then who does?"

Muir thought about it and then her face lit up. "Granny. They put Granny in as deputy mayor but told her that she'd never be able to act. They never took that away. Part of it, I think, was a threat against me."

"Do you know what you just said?" Burnie hugged her. "That means that she can request outside investigation." He was on his feet, pulling Muir with him, running for the stairs and then Muir's apartment.

They appeared in the midst of the four, no, five, as Dallas has appeared, breathless, startling them.

"Muir? What is going on?" Moira stared at her granddaughter.

"Granny? Did they ever remove you as deputy mayor?" Muir's words tumbled over one another.

"No, they didn't. I asked them to and they refused. Why?"

"Because Walter is in jail and unable to act. That makes you the mayor. I told Burnie that I think there was someone in the store when it burned down. You can call in outside investigators?"

"She can, Muir." Dallas had been listening closely. "We can look after that for her. Moira, we'll need a formal request from you."

"Then, how do I do that? And I want an investigation in Stewart Holman as well."

"We can look after that."

Chapter 12

Burnie looked up from his laptop the next morning, working on the balcony outside his home office. He closed his eyes, listening to the sounds of the early morning. This was when he wrote the best. He had been awake, he thought around two, finally rising and coming out to write. His characters were cooperating and he had put many words into the latest mystery he was authoring.

He frowned, hearing a faint tap, and then rose, heading back into his apartment, his laptop on his desk before he paced through to the front door. Hearing another soft tap, he opened it, to find Muir there, her face covered with tears. Burnie simply swept her into his arms and stood, Muir cradled tight to him as his prayer reached her ears.

"Muir? What happened, sweetheart?"

"Granny. I can't find her. Where is she?"

"What? You've looked through the apartment?"

"I have, Burnie. I haven't gone anywhere else. I was afraid to."

Burnie reached for his shoes and then her hand, closing his door behind him. "We'll go back through your apartment and then head downstairs. You didn't find a note?"

She shook her head. "I was too scared to look."

Burnie walked through the apartment, appearing back in the kitchen. "No sign of her. Let's head down to the lobby and then the chapel."

"You have a chapel?"

"We do. It's never locked." Burnie paused outside the chapel door, praying that Moira would be there. He gently shoved open the door. "There's Granny, Muir. She's found a place to pray."

Moira turned as the door open and then was on her feet, moving swiftly to gather Muir into her arms.

"Muir?"

"I was scared, Granny. I couldn't find you."

"I'm sorry, Muir. I thought I left a note for you on the kitchen counter."

Muir looked sheepish. "You might have. I didn't see it. I just panicked. I thought somehow Stewart had taken you."

"He hasn't. Now, sit, child. You too, Burnie. Let's pray this through as I taught you, Muir."

Muir nodded. "I know, Granny. I know. It's just that lately I didn't think God was hearing me."

"He has, child. He always has. Sometimes, it takes time for Him to work, but His timing is perfect. You wouldn't have been put here if you had left earlier. This is where we stand and fight."

"That's true, Granny. You've remembered something."

—

"I have, Muir. That's what had me out walking the building. The security guard was kind enough to show me this wonderful chapel. I didn't mean to scare you."

"I know, Granny. I know." Muir leaned back in Burnie's arms, not realizing that she had.

Moira shared a look with Burnie who simply shrugged.

Dallas turned from his phone, a troubled look on his face. Burnie had called, letting him know what had transpired that morning. He sighed. Another friend head over heels in love. How do we protect them this time, Lord? He rose and went looking for Will.

"Will? Got a moment?" Dallas tapped at Will's open door.

Will looked up, a smile on his face. "Sure, Dallas. Come on in. You look troubled." Will sat back in his chair.

"I am. It's this thing with Muir and her home village. I spoke with the provincial force. They'll be talking with Moira. They have been watching that village for a while now."

"Any particular reason why?"

"What we thought. Human trafficking. White slavery. The rumours that they are getting is that the teens and young women who are disappearing are shipped overseas."

"And that's what the plan was for Muir?" Will blew out a breath. "How do we keep that from happening?"

"That's what I am trying to think through. Burnie is fully involved. He doesn't have to say anything but he's in love."

"That just increases his danger. He'll put himself between Muir and anyone coming after her."

"He will. And we won't be able to talk him out of it. And she'll try her best to protect her grandmother." Dallas paused, thinking through the possibilities. "Walter was moved off today to eastern Ontario."

"That's good and also bad, I suspect. Muir will be blamed for that."

"She will." Dallas stood, his eyes on Will. "If you have any advice that you can give, please?"

Chapter 13

Standing outside of the library in town, Burnie watched as the unkempt man walked towards him and sighed. Stewart is in town and he's found me. Looking around, Burnie ducked back into the library and then through it, to exit from the employees' only door, and then around to his car, quickly disappearing into it and driving away. He pulled over and placed a call to Dallas, frustrated to get only his voice mail. He sighed, heading for home. He had done the research that he had needed to and now had to put that into his plot.

His mind on Muir, Burnie didn't see the vehicles that boxed him in until he was forced to slow down. He frowned. That's his game, is it? Burnie volunteered at a local driving school, teaching evasive maneuvers to the students. He watched closely, seeing that he had enough room to get around the car in front. He hit the accelerator as he pulled out and then flew past the car, slowing just enough to turn into a side road and then sped along it, heading for the back entrance to the Foundation grounds. Watching closely, he didn't see the cars, but figured that they would head for the front entrance.

The men in the two cars stared in disbelief as Burnie disappeared. This was not going well, the leader thought. Stewart will not be pleased, not at all. He wanted Burnie, to use as leverage against Muir and now that wasn't happening.

"How do we tell him?" The leader's companion finally spoke.

"I have no idea. I didn't think he would get away."

"Well, if you had done your research, you would have found out that he volunteers as a driving instructor. Stewart should have known that."

The leader snorted. "As if he'd bother looking into anything." He pulled to a stop and pointed to the door. "Out!"

"What do you mean?" His companion stared at him in disbelief.

"What I said. Out!" He barely waited for the door to close when he spun the wheel and headed back the way that he had just come and kept on going, heading for another province down east. He had had enough.

Burnie ran for the building after he had parked, fear in his heart for his lady. Muir was in the lobby, sitting with Ennis and Imly, and looked up as he slid to a halt near them.

"Burnie? What on earth?" Ennis stared at him.

"Muir? You're okay?"

"Of course, I am. It's you that doesn't seem to be."

"Just had an incident. I saw Stewart."

Muir paused, her eyes on him. "You did? Of course, you did. That's what he'd do. Come to town.

Send his men after you to get to me. Okay, so what do we do?"

"We do nothing, sweetheart. We wait. I don't know that we can do much right now."

Ennis and Imly shared a look before Imly spoke.

"Okay, Burnie. What would one of your characters do about now?"

Burnie began to laugh. "Imly, only you would ask that. Let me think." He was on his feet pacing.

"He does that, Muir, when he's thinking." Imly grinned at her. "He'll come up with a plan that will be so outrageous it will work."

"He came up with a logic problem for one of us." Ennis laughed at the remembrance. "It really did help."

"He did?" Muir was on her feet, standing in Burnie's way.

Burnie stopped abruptly, his hands out on Muir's arms to balance himself.

"Muir?"

"Burnie? What are you thinking?"

"What am I thinking? I'm not really sure. I am angry that he did what he did to you, that he showed up here today. I am angry that they tried to take me to use against you. That was their plan, more than likely."

"Anger doesn't help."

"No, it doesn't, and I'm praying my way through that." He turned her, an arm around her and led her to the conference room. "In here, sweetheart. This is where we plot and plan against the bad guys."

Muir stared at him. "Burnie? Really?"

He grinned. "Really. You're getting freer with how you talk to me."

Muir flushed. "I'm sorry. I didn't mean to." Her face shut down.

"Oh, sweetheart. Don't shut down on me. I like that."

She stared at him again. "You do? I was being obnoxious and impolite."

"Whoever told you that?"

"He did, when I would object to something."

"I'm not him. I want you to talk back to me. It's part of learning how to be human again. He had tried to drive that out of you."

Muir looked up at him, a surprised look on her face that turned to determination. "He did, didn't he? Burnie, will you teach me? Will you teach me how to live again?"

"That, sweetheart, would be an honour. And if it's something that the ladies or Granny or Anna can help you with, talk to them."

"I will." She surprised them both by suddenly hugging him before she turned and disappeared into the room.

———

Chapter 14

An hour later, Burnie looked up, surprised to see most of the men were in there, working away. He searched for Muir, a smile softening his face as he watched her sleep, her head down on her folded arms, as she sat in the chair next to him.

"She drifted off about forty-five minutes ago, Burnie." Brody looked up at him. "Her body's giving in."

"It is. She has been under so much stress. And the beatings that she took didn't help."

Brody stared at him, his mug slowly go back on the table. "Burnie? What are you talking about? What beatings?" His voice, though low, had grabbed the attention of the other men.

Burnie sighed, his eyes on Muir. "She was beaten, Brody, likely to break her spirit. She wasn't allowed outside of the store building unless she was told that she could be. I heard him talking to her. It was brutal, the language and the words." Burnie blinked rapidly as he looked up at Brody. "I know what the plan was. He didn't have to say it in words. The implication was there."

"Overseas?" Blair looked at him before looking at Muir, compassion on his face.

"That would be my guess. She wouldn't have survived."

"No, she wouldn't. And he'll be after her for revenge because she thwarted him. You too, Burnie." Brennen had moved to a chair beside Burnie. "So, how do we stop him?"

"For starters, Granny is now the mayor of that village. She is working with Dallas to bring in an outside force to investigate. His brother was the mayor but he's in custody for murder." Burnie's hand rested gently on Muir's back. "I fear for Granny. He'll try and stop the investigation."

"I'm sure he will." Baird spoke from where he was standing near the printer, his hands full of papers. "What else?"

Burnie drew a deep breath. "Muir thought that there was someone else in the building, someone who didn't make it out when the fire happened and then the propane tank exploded. Dallas is working on that."

"Murder?" Brendon nodded. "Of course, he would do that."

Buckley stood in the doorway, watching and listening before he spoke. "Burnie, how do you wish us to pray for you and for Muir?"

"For safety. For peace. For resolution of this. She asked me today to teach her how to live once more. I need prayer for that."

"And you have it, for all that. Let Locklin talk to her at some point. She may be able to help, given what our ministry is. This is when I miss being pastor of the church."

"But you are where God wants you. Maybe just for Muir." Burnie stood, gathering Muir into his arms. "I'll be back, fellows. I need to take my lady to Granny." He walked away, leaving them all staring after him.

"His lady? Granny?" Blair smiled. "He's found his family."

"That he has, just like some of us have with our wives' families. But we are still his family and as such, let's get to work. I don't want to see him go through what any of us did." Bradon dove back into his research, missing the looks that were exchanged.

Moira nodded as Burnie entered the apartment and pointed to the living room.

"In there, Burnie. That's where she's been sleeping." Moira reached to cover her granddaughter before she pointed back to the kitchen. "What happened?"

"We were working in the conference room and she dozed off. I gather she's not been sleeping?"

"No, I don't think so. I've been listening for her but she's quiet when she moves around at night. More so now than she used to be."

"That's from being held like she was."

"More than likely. Burnie? What did you go and do?" Granny searched his face.

"The fellows are working on solving this, Granny. It's what we've done for the others. They are successful." Burnie bit at his lip. "If we can talk to

—

you, find out everything that you can tell us, that will help."

"I can do that. How be you go get your laptop and work from here? And then I'll slip down and talk with them." Moira reached to hug Burnie. "Thank you, Burnie. You are bringing out my Muir again."

Burnie raised his head hours later, realizing that Moira had not returned, or if she had, he had not heard her. He watched as Muir sat up, brushing at the hair on her forehead and then rubbing at her eyes.

Muir jumped, realizing that she wasn't alone, her eyes huge as she stared at Burnie.

"Burnie? What are you going here?"

He grinned. "Writing. Watching you sleep. Did you have a good nap?"

She shook a finger at him. "Behave or I'll sic Granny on you. Where is she?"

"She was heading down to the conference room to talk to the fellows. She hasn't come back, not that I know." He sighed as he reached for his phone, having ignored it. He scrolled through his text messages. "She's still there. Brennen said that she has provided a wealth of information for them."

"That's good. She knows that village and the people." Muir stood, her feet tangling in her blanket for a moment before she shook it off. "I need to eat. I didn't get enough when I was working."

Burnie froze as he stood as well. "Muir? How often?"

"How often what? Burnie, you're not making sense." Muir looked over the fridge door at him.

"How often did you eat?"

She shrugged as she turned back to the fridge. "Once a day, twice if I behaved."

"Muir!"

"Burnie!" She echoed the sound of his voice. "There wasn't a lot I could do. I tried at first to get more, but that just had me deprived of meals for days on end."

Burnie simply shut the fridge door and gathered her into a hug, startling her.

"Burnie, you need to warn me."

"What? Warn you when I want to hug you? Then I give you fair warning now. It will happen and happen a lot." He grinned down at the outrage on her face. "You need this, Muir."

"I do?" She sounded disgruntled. "I also need to eat."

Chapter 15

Moira looked up at last, her eyes on Barnabas as he stood speaking with Breck. He's the one I need to speak with, she thought. And I will, at some point. He needs to know Muir's history and I guess I need to talk to both Muir and Burnie. She has never known her full history or why I had such trouble leaving the village.

Barnabas turned at that moment, finding Moira watching him. He spoke with Breck for a few more moments and then walked towards her, detouring to fix her a cup of tea and himself his inevitable mug of coffee.

"Moira? How are you?" He sat beside her, his attention focused on her.

"Barnabas? To tell you the truth, I'm not sure. But I do need to talk with you. There are some things that even Muir does not know about her history"

"There is? Shouldn't you be speaking with her?"

"I will. With both Muir and Burnie. They're a couple, whether they acknowledge it or not. He's good for her and she's good for him." Moira stared down at her clasped hands. "I don't want what I have to say to tarnish Muir."

"It won't, Moira. It won't. You've met our ladies here. You know that we treat them just as that, as ladies."

"I know." Moira sighed. "Muir never knew her parents. We have emigrated from Ireland just before Muir was born. When she was about nine months old, her parents had to return to Ireland for business reasons. There was a plane crash into the Atlantic Ocean and they were killed. There were in fact no survivors. The authorities assumed that they had crashed. But there was always a question about that."

"We can look into that. I have a friend who can do that. Just let me have all the details and I will send it on for you."

"You would do that?"

"I would, Moira. I would. You need this closure as well. You have always questioned it, have you not?"

"I have." Moira blinked for a moment to clear the moisture from her eyes. "Bless you, Barnabas. Now, as to the village. Stewart Holman was not the original owner of the store. My son had been. During my grief, he moved in, forged documents and took it over. I tried to fight him but he threatened to have me declared incompetent and take Muir away from me. I couldn't allow that.

"As she grew, I would find him watching her. Not in an appropriate way, I would add. When his brother became mayor, they decided that I would be deputy mayor. They laughed at me when I refused, stating that I had no choice. They once more threatened Muir. They were never specific with their threats."

Barnabas looked past her for a moment, watching at Burnie and Muir stood behind her, Muir tight in Burnie's arms.

"What else, Moira?"

"I tried to leave but was prevented on so many occasions. The village is mostly his friends and relatives. I wanted to get Muir away. There was no work, other than for the store. It was fine at first, but then Muir become more distant and troubled. She was finally able to arrange for a stranger to take me with him, hidden in his car. I am sure that she suffered for that."

"I am sure that she did. Where did you go? To where we found you?"

"I did. I didn't want to go somewhere that Muir could not find me. The man had willingly helped us, made her memorize the address and not write it down. He was only there for about thirty minutes, and we took advantage of that. We had nothing that we wanted to bring with us."

"That's sad, Moira." Barnabas reached to hug her. "Now, I will take this information that you have given me and speak with my friend." He looked behind her once more. "Muir and Burnie are right behind you. They have heard what you had to say."

"They have?" Moira's eyes slid closed. "There is so much to tell Muir that I don't know where to start."

"Start by telling her that you love her. That you loved her father and mother. That you tried your best to get her free of the village and the control there. Talk it over with her and with Burnie. I don't think that Burnie is walking out of her life." Barnabas reached to hug her before he rose, his hand resting on Burnie's shoulder before he walked away.

"Granny?" Muir's voice was barely audible.

"Muir, my love. I'm sorry. I should have spoke with you earlier." Moira was on her feet, her beloved granddaughter in her arms.

"No, you couldn't, Granny. Now, you can. We're free of that village. These men are working to ensure that. Granny?" Muir touched the tears on her grandmother's face. "Can we go and talk?"

"We can."

Burnie stood back, not sure where to be. Muir saw his hesitation and reached for his hand, including him in her family and the discussion that would follow.

Chapter 16

Burnie walked the paths around the building that evening, twilight coming down on him as he did so. He was troubled, that much he knew, by what Moira had told him and Muir. She had added to what she had told Barnabas. He turned as he heard a sound behind him, an arm up to deflect the blow aimed for his head and then staggered at a knife slashed at his abdomen. He went down, his foot kicking out in a desperate move to stop his assailant before a blow to the head rendered him senseless.

The man stood over him, before a sound caught at his ear. He turned and then ran for the woods, anger building in him that he had not been able to take Burnie with him. He would need to return. Stewart would not be happy with him, that much he knew.

Kade gave a low growl, staring off into the woods. Bradon stopped, puzzled, before he shrugged, calling Kade to follow him. Kade's attention went then to the huddled form in front of them. With a bark, he had forged ahead, his nose nudging at Burnie's face.

"Burnie?" Bradon was on his knees, his hands feeling for a pulse. Relief coursed through him before he had Burnie up and over his shoulder, heading for the well-stocked infirmary in the building.

Brady stared at Bradon for a moment as he watched him heading for the infirmary before he was running after him, his work duffel bag dropped at the door. Brady had been one that Bradon intended to call, a paramedic who willingly stepped in to help his friends.

"Bradon?"

"It's Burnie. Kade and I found him. I think that it just happened. He's taken a blow to the head, but it's the abdomen I'm worried about. He's been slashed across it."

Brady had reached for the scissors, slicing through Burnie's shirt and T-shirt. He grimaced as he saw the wound.

"I'll need your help, Bradon. Is Doc around?"

"He should be. I saw him about an hour ago. He said that he was planning on being home, he had some Bible study that he wanted to do."

"Okay. Find him."

Bradon was off on a run, his quiet command to Kade keeping the dog in the room, his eyes on Burnie.

"What happened, Kade? Did you see it?" Brady spoke quietly to the dog, even as he worked to clean around the wound. He drew a breath of relief. It wasn't quite as bad as he had initially thought.

"What do you have, Brady?" Doc's voice startled him for a moment, and he heard Bradon call Kade back.

"Burnie has a slash across his abdomen. Not as bad as I thought. And I haven't had a chance to check his head. Bradon said he had been hit."

"Okay, let's take a look." Doc looked around. "Bradon? Muir?"

"I'll go find her and Moira."

"I think they were heading for the chapel, if I heard Anna correctly. The ladies were meeting tonight."

"Oh, okay. I'll head there."

Bradon hesitated just inside the door that he had opened quietly, watching as the ladies had their heads bowed in prayer. Ennis had looked up and then moved towards him, following him as he exited the room.

"Bradon?" Her voice held a question.

"I didn't see Muir. Is she here?"

"She is. She's on the other side of Fynn. Moira's beside her. Do you need her?"

"I do. Burnie's been hurt and Doc wants her with him."

"Oh, no! Let me go get her." Ennis was back in short order, Muir almost running from the room, Moira hurrying after her.

"Bradon? Ennis said Burnie was hurt." Muir was frightened that he had been badly hurt, but was afraid to ask.

"I didn't mean to frighten you, Muir. He's here in our infirmary. Doc and Brady are with him. Let's get you to him." He paused, a thought crossing his mind. "Are you afraid of blood?"

"Blood? No, not that I am aware of." Muir ran ahead of him, shoving open the door, and then coming to a halt beside Doc. "Doc?"

"Muir? You can handle blood?"

"I can. What can I do?"

"Just step around me to the head of the bed. He's starting to rouse and keeps asking for you. I need you to calm him down while I finish with this."

Muir moved to stand by Burnie, a hand reaching out to touch his face. Burnie turned into her hand, his eyes flickering open and closed.

"I need to get up. I need to find Muir." He struggled to rise, despite the admonitions of Doc. Bradon moved into help hold him down.

"Talk to him, Muir." Brady glanced up at her before his attention went back to Doc. "Stitches?"

Doc shook his head. "Just a couple where it's the deepest. Has anyone called it in?"

"I did, Doc." Bradon shot him a look. "Dallas is on his way out. He said he was heading this way anyway."

"Muir? I need to find Muir?"

"I'm right here, Burnie. Now, please lie still." Muir bent over him, coming into his line of sight.

"Muir? You're okay? They didn't hurt you?" Burnie's eyes slid closed even as pain crossed his face.

Chapter 17

Burnie's arm over his shoulder, Brady moved slowly into the bedroom that Moira pointed him to. She had just refused to let Burnie go back to his own apartment, insisting instead that she would look after him. Burnie sat for a moment on the side of the bed, an arm wrapped around his middle, his head down before he nodded at Brady's quiet question asking if he was okay.

"I think so, Brady. Thanks."

"Then, let's get you horizontal." Brady helped him before reaching to pull off his sneakers.

Moira was there, pulling up the covers, a gentle hand touching his head before she turned and pointed to the door.

"I'll call you or Doc, Brady. Thank you." She reached to hug the young man. "Go on, now. You're just off shift, aren't you?"

"I am." He grinned at her use of words. "You're a quick learner."

Moira smiled at him. "I always have been. Stop by in the morning."

"I will." Brady stopped to hug Muir, much to her surprise. "He'll be okay, Muir. Doc said that."

"I know. I'm just worried."

"We know you are. You are in our prayers."

"Thank you." Muir disappeared down the hall, to stand in the bedroom doorway watching Burnie before she moved to sit beside the bed, her hand on his shoulder. Exhaustion got the best of her at last, and her head went down on the pillow, her hair just touching his cheek.

Thirty minutes later, Breck stood and watched, listening to Moira's quiet comments. He had been out when the event had happened and had just returned, coming quickly to see what he could do for the two ladies.

"Here, let me move Muir." He reached to gently lift her, turning towards the door.

"The living room, Breck. She's been sleeping on the sofa there."

"She has? That's unusual?" Breck tucked a pillow under Muir's head even as Moira covered her granddaughter with a soft yellow blanket.

Moira pointed to the kitchen. "There's coffee on. I expected some of you fellows would be through."

"They would have been, but Brady sent out a group text to us all."

"He did? How does that work?"

"It's a text message that goes to all of us. And we respond when we get it. I just got mine as I was coming in. I had had my phone turned off."

"Oh, I see." Moira hesitated. "Did you have your dinner, then?"

"I didn't." He went to protest as Moira reached for a bowl and then the soup, making him a sandwich to go with it. "Thank you, Moira. I didn't expect this."

"No, you didn't. And you would never ask." Moira sat near him, her tea cup on the table, her hands wrapped around it. "Brady never said what happened."

Breck wiped his mouth on the cloth napkin, fingering it as he studied the older lady. "I didn't get a lot of the details, other than Bradon and Kade found Burnie outside with knife wound and a head wound."

"He was walking by himself?"

"He was. He does that. He says it helps to clear his head. His characters also talk to him when he's doing that."

"They do? That's an interesting thought." Moira turned her head to listen before she looked back at Breck. "Breck, you were there when I spoke to Barnabas. Do you know if there is any news?"

"I don't think so. Emma, our friend that he was speaking of, did get back to us. She's working on it, but she had a priority investigation that she was working on."

"I understand. I don't expect her to find out much, not after twenty-seven years."

"It's a long time to wonder, Moira. We'll do what we can to find out for you and Muir."

"Thank you, Breck." Moira rose to clear away his dishes, stopping as his hands reached to them.

"I'll do them, Moira. And then I'm taking my mug of coffee, heading in for that nice comfortable easy chair and spending the night here. You may need help with Burnie."

Moira reached to hug him again. "I just might. There are towels and whatnot in the bathroom of that bedroom. I'll find a blanket for you. God bless you, Breck. And why have you not found your lady yet?"

Her question shocked Breck into silence before he smiled. She's out there somewhere, isn't she, Lord? I just have not found her yet. I pray for my friend and his lady. Please, dear Lord, protect them. Help us to find what we need to bring these men to justice and please prevent Burnie and his lady from going through what some of the others have.

Chapter 18

Early the next morning, Burnie roused, his head coming up from the pillow as he stared around the dimly-lit room, before he sat on the side of the bed, one arm wrapping around his middle, the other hand on his head. He searched for his shoes, finding them, and grimacing with pain as he bent over to shove his feet into them. That he wasn't in his own apartment, he knew. He just wasn't sure where he was.

Stumbling somewhat as he walked through the hallway, he kept his focus on the door, opening it and peeking out before he closed it behind him.

"There's my apartment. But whose was I in and why?" He shut the door to his own place behind him, kicking off his shoes and then heading for his bed. He could barely keep his eyes open. Pulling the covers over him, Burnie was soon asleep again, knowing that he had to be up soon to work on his manuscript. He was now on a deadline with it and needed to finish it.

Muir had raised her head when she heard Burnie closing the door and then had risen herself, standing in the bedroom doorway and not seeing him. She sighed. Where did he go, Lord? She reached for a blanket to wrap around herself and headed for Burnie's door, thinking that was where he was. Fatigue soon had her sitting on the floor, wrapped in the blanket, her head against his door.

Doc paused the next morning as he approached Burnie's, a frown on his face before he shook his head. Burnie must have gone home, Doc thought, before he bent to draw Muir to her feet.

"Muir? How long have you been out here?"

Muir rubbed at her eyes and then squinted at Doc. "I'm not sure. Burnie came home and I wanted to make sure that I didn't miss him leaving again."

"Here, young lady. Let's get you back to your home." Doc persisted in leading her there, despite her reluctance to do that. "I'll come find you. In you go. Breck? You're here?"

"I am, Doc. I can't find Burnie, though."

"He's at home. I found Muir sleeping against his door. Make sure she had her tea and something to eat. I'll be back."

Doc tapped at Burnie's door, then twisted the knob, shaking his head at finding the door opening. He quietly called for Burnie as he entered before he walked through, searching for him. He stood at the bedroom doorway, watching as Burnie slept, before he approached him and then shook him gently awake.

"Burnie? Can you wake up for me?"

Burnie frowned at Doc's voice. "Doc? What are you going here?"

"Looking for you. I left you in Moira's care last night but I find you at home. Did you let her know that you were leaving?"

Burnie stared at him. "Why would you do that?" He groaned as he sat up. "My abdomen hurts. So does my head."

"You don't remember? You were hit over the head and slashed across your upper abdomen. Brady and I put in a couple of stitches to the wound. How are you feeling?"

"I have no idea how I am supposed to feel." Burnie groaned. "I'm sorry, Doc. I didn't mean to sound like that."

"I know you didn't. Let me have a listen to your heart and lungs and then check out your wound. I found a young lady wrapped up in a blanket, sleeping against your door just a few moments ago."

Burnie watched him, and then sighed. "Muir? She did that?"

"She did, Burnie. She was that concerned, I suspect, when she couldn't find you. She wouldn't have tried to enter your place."

"She was? I need to find her." Doc's hand on his shoulder kept Burnie in place. "Doc?"

"She's at home. Breck was there as is her grandmother. I would suggest that we get you cleaned up. You're still in the clothes Bradon found you in."

"I am?" Burnie stared down at himself. "I don't remember what happened."

"Kade and Bradon found you outside, down on the ground. Kade alerted to something but Bradon called him off, not seeing anything himself. Come on, son. On your feet."

85

Showered, shaved, in clean clothes, and feeling refreshed, Burnie moved slowly towards the entrance door, Doc's hand on his back.

"Muir is okay?"

"She is, other than being worried about you." Doc closed the door behind him and then moved the few feet to Muir's door, finding Breck waiting outside for them. "Breck?"

"Doc. Burnie. How is he, Doc?"

"I'm fine, Breck. Any reason that you're standing out here?"

Breck just grinned and shook his head, standing to one side at Burnie glared at him before moving past him and soundly shutting the door behind him.

"You shouldn't have done that, Breck." Doc shook a finger at him, all the while grinning himself.

"I know. I just couldn't help myself. Muir is wandering the apartment, still wrapped in a blanket." Breck shook his head. "She's that worried."

"I know that she is. We'll need to see what we can do to help her out." Doc paused before he too entered the apartment, Breck staring after him before he walked away.

"Barnabas?" Breck tapped at his friend's office door, not surprised to find him there already.

"Breck? You're up early." Barnabas pointed to a chair.

"I am. I stayed at Muir's last night as Burnie was there. Only Burnie left in the middle of the night. Muir followed him. Doc found her sleeping against Burnie's door this morning."

"He did? Is she that worried?"

"She is worried, but I think there's more. Burnie is her lifeline right now to reality and to getting back to who she is."

"He is. So, what do we do? The fellows are working on his adventure as they can?"

"They are." Breck was quiet, his eyes on his hands that he was rubbing together, an uncharacteristic move for him. "Who do we question about this, Barnabas? Dallas is trying his best, but he's tied up with his other cases. Moira has talked to the police force who will be investigating but she says that will take months. Muir doesn't have months."

"No, she doesn't. Emma is working on finding out what happened to Muir's parents but since it's so long ago, she's needing to do some deep research."

"That's what worries me, Barnabas. I don't think either Muir or Brady have months."

Chapter 19

The next day, Burnie raised his head from his work, a frown on his face. He had just completed the rough draft of his manuscript and needed a break. He rose, stretching, a hand to his abdomen as he grimaced with pain. His headache had returned in full force, and he had been fighting himself against taking anything. Burnie turned as he heard soft sounds from the kitchen and then a smile lit up his face.

"Muir." His whisper didn't go far.

Burnie smiled as he remembered her that morning, frowning at him adorably as she had shoved him from her apartment back to his and then down the hallway to his office, forcing him down into his chair.

"You need to work, Burnie. You have a deadline, don't you?"

"I do, Muir, but it's not for a week yet for the rough draft." He grinned up at her.

"But, you need to finish it now. Who knows what tomorrow or the next day will bring that will prevent you from finishing." Muir had paced his office, her hands on her cheeks.

Burnie had been content to watch her, wishing that he dared speak from his heart. He could envision her in his apartment all the time. But she's not ready yet, is she, Lord? I won't rush her. I know my friends married quickly but I just can't do that to her. She needs to have this time, to relearn how to live and to learn to enjoy life. If it means she moves on, dear Lord, then I must let her.

He stood in the kitchen doorway, watching as Muir worked away, not quite sure what she was doing. He finally approached and stood behind her, watching over her shoulder as she prepared sandwiches, muttering away to herself as she did so.

"Those look delicious, Muir." He reached around her to snag a piece of cucumber, earning himself a smack on his fingers as he did so.

"No snacking. You'll ruin your lunch." Muir paused, horrified at what she had done before she spun, a hand to her mouth as she opened it to apologize.

Burnie simply shook his head. "You are quite right, Muir. I shouldn't have helped myself." He grinned. "But it was just so tempting, sitting there. And the sandwiches do look good. You are joining me, are you not?"

Muir hesitated, not sure if she should or not. "I was hoping that I could, Burnie." Her eyes sought his and she once more found that look in his eyes, that said she was special and wonderful and that he cared for her.

Burnie simply reached to hug her, a kiss on her forehead, before he stood, just waiting for what, he wasn't sure. He felt Muir move and then her arms come around him even as her head laid against his chest, over his heart.

"Burnie?" He could hear the question in her voice.

"Muir? I know it's too soon. You need to enjoy life, to find what you haven't had. I don't want to take that from you. But I care for you, deeply. At some point, if you are willing, I would like to date you, to see where our friendship goes."

Muir had raised her head to look at him. "Just how long will you give me?"

"As long as it takes, sweetheart. As long as it takes."

Muir nodded before she spoke. "We need to eat, Burnie. I need to think over what you have said and pray about it."

"I know that you do. Talk to Granny. Or any of the ladies, if you feel you can."

"I might. Locklin seems to be willing to do that." Muir moved from him, to set their meal on the table, sitting herself beside Burnie, not surprised when he reached for her hand as he asked the blessing.

Moira watched her granddaughter later that afternoon, finding her quieter than normal. She sighed. Burnie? What did you go and do? Lord, this child needs You so much right now. We need to work with her, to teach her that she is free and help her to find the peace and joy that she has lost.

"Muir, child?" Moira wrapped an arm around her and drew her down to the sofa, as she called it. "What happened?"

Muir blinked, coming back from her thoughts and the dreams that she had buried.

"Burnie kissed me, Granny, on my forehead. He wants to date me." She sounded surprised, yet hopeful.

"He did, did he? And?"

"And?" Muir turned to her grandmother.

"And is he?"

"Not yet. I asked for time to pray about it."

"You did? Thank you, Muir, for not rushing into anything." Moira hugged her granddaughter.

"He told me to talk to you, to any of the other ladies."

"That sounds like a wonderful idea, child. I have been talking with them, learning their stories. They all have such different ones, even though they do sound similar. When the ones married quickly, it was to protect them, they said. The men have all stated to me that they knew when they saw their ladies that they were the ones God meant for them."

"I didn't think there was such a thing as love at first sight." Muir's voice was quiet.

"There is, child. And I would say Burnie is one of those men too."

The ladies sat in silence for a while, each busy with their own thoughts.

"Granny? How do I know?"

"How? Pray and ask God to show you His plans for you. We are working with you, to teach you once

—

more how to live and love and have that joy and peace that disappeared from you."

"I know, Granny. I know that you are. I just don't know how I will ever know."

Chapter 20

Two days later, Brennen looked up from his computer in the conference room, searching the room, before he rose.

"Brandon? Did you see this?" He held out a sheet of paper that he had detoured by the printer to retrieve.

"What's that?" Bradon looked up, distracted, before he reached for it to read it. "Is this for real?"

"It is. It says that Holman was in Ireland when Muir's parents were to be there. That sounds strange."

"It does. Moira never said anything about that." Brandon was on his feet, heading for the door. "We need to talk with her."

"We will but she's not home. She headed into town with Anna and Locklin."

"Oh. Then I guess we can't." Brandon turned back, a frown on his face. "Do you think that he had something to do with the plane?"

"That's my thought. I know it was a small executive-class plane. With only the pilots and Muir's parents. Whoever it was that arranged for them to return to Ireland set it up."

"Set it up?" Brendon spoke from behind Brennen. "That's an interesting choice of words."

"Because I think that's exactly what happened." Brennen stared down at his feet. "I found news articles about Holman and his link to the company in Ireland."

"You did? I don't like that." Brady spoke up from where he sat. "How do we prove what we think?"

"More research and investigation. It may mean someone will have to head over there." Branigan looked up. "I think that I found a link to that as well."

"We need to bring Burnie in on this." Blair was on his feet. "I talked to him earlier. He was heading into his office down here to work on his last manuscript."

Burnie stood just inside the door, his eyes on his friends, thinking back over the years. Barnabas had approached each one of the men, offering them employment with the Barnabas Foundation, an organization set up to serve as a source of encouragement for others. Each of the men were orphans, each from a different province, and they all shared the same initials as Barnabas. The Foundation paid the men their wages, letting their employers free up that money to hire others without worrying about finding the finances necessary to do so. The Foundation itself was named for Barnabas, but also for the Barnabas in the Bible, who served as an encourager to the apostle Paul.

"Blair? You were looking for me?" Burnie's question broke through the quiet chatter.

"I was. We have some information that we need to go over with you." Blair beckoned him over.

"And I have some information for you. I've been receiving some nasty messages in the last couple of days, since I was hurt. I spoke with Dallas. He's heading out this way later. Will is sending him." Burnie sank into a chair, fatigue gnawing at him. He had been unable to sleep the night before, his headache keeping him awake, as well as his worry about Muir.

"Where's Muir?" Benen looked around, a question on his face.

"With Berneen and Cadee. They've decided that they needed to pray with her on a daily basis. I'm glad."

"That's good. Now, where do we go?" Benen looked down at his work. "I think I'm just making a mess, is what I'm doing."

"We need to start using the whiteboards, fellows. And combine what we're finding. I'm sure there is overlapping." Brody moved to start with what he had found. "Burnie, want to set up a logic problem again?"

Burnie nodded, wishing that he had not done just that. "We can, once we start finding out more."

"I think we can start now." Brady's hand on his shoulder kept him in his chair. "You sit there and direct me. I'll get started."

Two hours later, Muir peeked around the door that she had opened, Berneen and Cadee behind her, before they entered, trays of sandwiches and fruit in their hands. Berneen and Cadee worked away to set it up, Muir standing watching in amazement the concentration going on around the room.

"It's how they work, Muir." Cadee grinned at her. "It's a wonder to see them still like this. All of them are athletes and spend time in the gym or out on the track running."

"They do? I haven't seen the gym yet. I would be interested in doing that. I've never seen one."

Berneen stared at her. "We have been remiss. Tomorrow, Muir, we'll do a field trip. Fynn also has a building full of creepy-crawlies that she would love to show you. Hagen has a woodworking shop attached to the gym."

"Wow! All that? And where's your library?"

Berneen and Cadee stared at one another.

"That is one thing that we have never thought about. We should set up one." Cadee reached to hug Muir. "I nominate you to run it."

"Oh, I couldn't do that. I'm not educated." Muir kept her eyes down, not wanting to see the pity in them.

"That wouldn't matter, Muir. If it's what you want to do, and you want to go to school for it, Barnabas will have the Foundation sponsor you."

"Oh, they can't do that!" Muir was horrified.

"They can and they will, Muir. Pray about it." Berneen hugged her before moving off to find Baird.

"They would?"

"They would, Muir. Each one of us ladies have a wage through them. They are encouragers that way. We can work, volunteer, be a student, or not, depending on where we want to go with our lives. I'm working through a nursing program."

"You are?" Muir became quiet. "I'm not that good. I mean, I had good marks through school but I'm not good enough to do anything like that." She jumped as she felt arms come around her.

"You are, Muir. You are right up there with the other ladies. God is working in you. I can see the change. You don't have to rush into anything. And I think you would do wonders with a library." Burnie dropped a kiss on her cheek, causing her to blush.

"You think so?" She turned to find herself almost nose to nose with him.

"I do, sweetheart. I do." He dropped a kiss on her nose. "Come, let's eat and then I'll walk you through everything that we've been working on today and yesterday." He nodded through the boards. "That's only part of it."

Muir's eyes grew round. "That? That's us?"

"It is, Muir. It is. And our friend has sent on a whole raft of material that we need to sort through."

"She has? I can't afford to pay her." Muir grew distraught at the very thought of how much it would cost.

Burnie sighed, realizing that they had overlooked something with Muir. He resolved to not let it happen again.

"She won't charge us, Muir. She never charges a friend, and she considers us and the ladies all friends. In fact, she has asked to meet you."

"She has? Why?"

"Because you're special to me, and because you're part of the Foundation family."

Chapter 21

Moira watched as Muir curled up in the corner of the sofa that night, a frown on her face before she began to pray for her granddaughter. Something had happened that day, she decided, and Muir was unsure of how to deal with it.

"Muir? Can we pray?" Moira sat beside her, reaching for Muir's hand.

"We can, Granny. I'm so conflicted, I think you would say. We need to talk, but we need to pray more."

Muir finally raised her head, her hand still tight in her grandmother's, feeling a peace once more in her heart, a peace that she had not felt in years. She reached to hug her Granny, hanging on tighter than she had been.

"Thank you, Granny. I needed that prayer. I always like to think of how Christ prayed for us but I had forgotten."

"You may have forgotten, but you are not forgotten. You have many here praying for you. I talked to young Buckley this morning. He stated that the church they attend have you and Burnie on what they call their prayer chain. Just asking for protection and a solution. He said the people don't need a lot of details in order to pray."

"I think that I have felt those prayers. I have felt someone watching me when I'm outside, and that scares me. I have talked to the security guard. He is willing to go outside with me."

"That's a smart move you made, child. I wouldn't have thought of it."

Muir's head went down on her Granny's shoulder. "I hadn't, not really. I was going outside today and he was at the door. I think he saw that I was hesitating and offered to go with me. That gave me peace, Granny. Is that the Lord teaching me to think and live again?"

"I am sure it is. God will teach you to live again. I can see the change already. Young Burnie is good for you."

"He is, Granny. I am still praying through what he asked."

"He doesn't want you to rush into anything and then regret it. I've seen how he watches you, child. He is in love with you, and not quite sure how to tell you."

"He is? He said he wanted me to learn to live again, to enjoy this time. I wouldn't be able to if he's not in it."

"You're falling in love, Muir. I wish your parents were here to share this with you." Moira stopped to wipe at a tear that trickled down her cheek.

"Do you really think that they are dead, Granny?"

"I always thought that but there has always been a question. I thought it was because they couldn't find the plane."

"Burnie said his friend is working on that. She wants to come and meet me." Muir sat up. "Granny, I just remembered. Stewart was talking with someone one day. I wasn't supposed to be near him but I had to clean the shelves. He said something about Mom and Dad. That he was sure that they wouldn't give in."

"He said that? Did you tell Burnie?"

"No, I just remembered it. Can it be that they might still be alive?"

"It might. We'll get Burnie to sort it out for you." Moira grew quiet, a prayer in her heart for Muir. "Muir, I regret that I let you work for Stewart, but I can see that God was at work. We would never have been able to leave the village if you hadn't been there and approached that man."

"What happened to him?"

"I don't know. He dropped me off at that apartment and then just disappeared. I never saw him afterwards at all."

"An angel." Muir's voice was low.

"It could be, Muir. It could be. Now, we need to do some planning. We need to look after that wardrobe of yours and mine. Barnabas has assured me that the Foundation will fund it for us."

"They will? They are so wonderful." Muir looked up as a tap came to the door and then Burnie appeared. "Burnie?"

"Muir?" He grinned at her before he sat in Moira's favourite chair.

"How are you feeling, Burnie?" Moira shook her head at him.

"Better than I was. I think working in the conference room has helped. The headache, or rather that one, has disappeared."

"Which one hasn't?" Muir frowned at him.

Burnie grinned again, a sparkle of mischief on his face. "The one where Muir has not agreed to go out to dinner with me."

Chapter 22

Turning from the whiteboards the next morning, Burnie frowned, a thought crossing his mind. He pulled out his phone and scrolled through his messages. It was as he had thought. He was beginning to get the text messages threatening him. Only the threats were vague. He looked up as he heard footsteps stop in front of him.

"Dallas? How'd you do that?"

"Do what?" Dallas was puzzled.

"Appear just as I needed to speak with you." Burnie held out his phone. "You need to see these."

"Messages?" Dallas took his phone, scrolling through them, sending the ones he needed to on to the crime lab.

"Those ones. Muir refuses a phone. I've tried to talk her into one."

"No talking into it, Burnie. Just give her one. Tell her the police have asked that she have one. Or I can do it."

"It might be better coming from you. It would have more weight." Burnie stared at his friend. "You're here for a reason."

"I am." Dallas frowned as he stared around. "Where is everyone?"

"At work. I have to head that way soon." Burnie nodded at the boards. "This is what we have so far."

Dallas wandered along the walls, reading the boards, taking notes as he needed to.

"It never fails to amaze me how you all find this information. You don't have access to the sites and programs that I do."

"I know we don't. I would say it's God that is leading. What can you tell me?"

"Right at the moment?" Dallas grinned for a moment, the look of worry and care dropping from his face. "We're working on Holman and his brother. Emma has found a wealth of information that she is couriering over today, she said. She specifically mentioned Muir's parents."

"She did? Muir and Moira are wondering if they are still alive, if the plane wreck was staged."

"That we are looking at. I talked to Barnabas. He said something about sending a couple of the fellows over there like he did before."

"He did mention it in passing but we haven't heard yet who he wants to send."

"He didn't say." Dallas turned to lean against a table, his eyes on the whiteboards. "Burnie? What is your feeling on all this?"

"My feeling? That Muir was being beaten down so that she would not make any trouble when she was sent overseas. That she would just do what she was told and not fight them. I hate to think of how she had lived in the last six months or so since Granny moved away. She hasn't said a whole lot but I heard him, Dallas. He was brutal and didn't really care how he talked to her. She just stood there, her head down and took it. Her spirit was almost broken. That's what he did to her." Dallas frowned. "He was no amateur, Dallas. He was too smooth and good at what he was doing."

"I see. And the beatings? Has she said much?"

Burnie shook his head. "It's as if she's ashamed that it happened, that she wants to forget them. But she never will. I am praying that she will learn to let God handle that for her. Granny says that she's sleeping on the couch, not in her own bed."

"She is? Because of?" Dallas didn't finish his question, not quite sure how to.

"I think that she is afraid. She told me once that she didn't really have a bed at the store, just a small pallet. He refused to let her go home, told her that she couldn't when he employed her. She managed to get away when Granny was there but once Granny was gone, he locked her in the store and refused to let her leave. She doesn't know what happened to the home that they had. Granny owned it."

"I'll look into it. Sounds as if we have him from kidnapping, physical and mental abuse, unlawful confinement."

"At the very least." Burnie grew silent, his eyes on the floor as he thought through what he knew. "I am sure that he is the one who started the fire in the store. He didn't like that I stood up to him for Muir."

"You did? You have not mentioned that."

"I didn't? I thought I had. I guess with the explosion and all, I just sort of forgot it. I know that I stepped between them, refusing to let him hit her. The look of hatred was horrible. He disappeared and it was shortly afterwards that we smelled smoke and saw the flames. He must have done something to the tank to cause it to explode. The fire wasn't near it, not from what I can remember." He slanted a look at Dallas. "How much investigation didn't happen?"

"All of it. There was no investigation and when the other force went in, the store site had been completely cleared away."

"Hiding the evidence? That makes sense. Muir was worried about someone else being there."

"I know. But unfortunately we can't prove or disprove that. Not unless someone talks and then tells us where the debris would be." Dallas turned as he heard a sound beside him. "Muir?"

Burnie took one look at her distressed face and wrapped her into his arms. "Muir?"

"Dallas, there's a ravine outside of town. Look there. He's claimed that he has dumped people there. We just thought it was talk."

"We'll do that, Muir. But first, I need to give you this." Dallas held out a phone, finding her shaking her head at him.

"No, I don't want one."

"But you see, Muir, it has now become a necessity. I have been told that you will take this and

106

keep it on you." He gave her no choice but to take it. "That order comes from the chief, Will Peters. He has insisted that you take it. He programmed in every number that he could think of that you might need." Dallas showed her how to operate the phone.

Muir stared down at it. "I don't like it. But I will keep it with me. How do you turn off the sound?"

Burnie gave a quick grin that he hid. "You don't want to do that, Muir. You need to be able to hear it ring."

"I know. I just don't want to." She walked away, leaving the two men staring after her.

Chapter 23

Muir stared at the phone that she had set on the table in their kitchen, a finger lightly poking at it. She sighed. This was not what she wanted. She had heard the other ladies talking about how they had received messages that were brutal and nasty, and she wanted no part of that. She felt her grandmother's hand on her head and then heard the chair beside as it slid back to let Moira sit.

"Muir?" Moira watched her closely. "Is that phone going to bite you or something?"

"It's the something that I am afraid of, Granny." Muir looked up at the ceiling, a bleak look around her eyes. "What if Stewart finds out the number? Can he track me?"

"I am sure that Will Peters would have ensured that the number was private and not available to just anyone. I met him the other day, Muir, when I was at the church with Locklin. He was troubled about you."

"He was? I haven't met him, so why would he be?"

"Because you're a young lady in trouble. Because you're friends with Burnie, and possibly something more to him. Because, as he put it, we're part of the Foundation family now and he looks after them, just as he does anyone else in the area."

"He said that?" Muir's eyes turned to Moira. "We never had that, Granny. We always felt threatened by the officers in our home village."

"I know, Muir. And that should not have been. Stewart was not working on his own, of that I am sure. He didn't have the smarts to set up the network of disappearances that happened."

"There were others, weren't there?" Muir's voice was barely above a whisper. "I remember two of the girls, just mid-teens, who disappeared. Their parents never said a word, but they looked so sad and beaten down. Where did he send them?"

"I don't know, Muir. We need to give the names to that young Dallas or to Breck. Maybe they can discover something."

"He almost succeeded, Granny."

"Who?"

"Stewart. He almost succeeded in breaking me. If Burnie hadn't stepped in and helped me, I would not have been able to resist whatever it was that Stewart had planned. I was ready to just give up."

"I know, child. I know. I am thankful that God provided a way for you to escape." Moira reached to hug Muir, holding on for longer than she normally did. When she sat back, she studied Muir. "Muir? You are healing. There is no rush to decide what you need to do for the rest of your life."

"I know, Granny, but I feel so useless. I need to be doing something, but I'm not sure what."

"Talk to Burnie. Or talk to one of the ladies."

"I have talked to Devaney and Ennis. They told me to talk to Locklin, but I don't know her well enough to do that."

"That will not matter to her, Muir. If you wish, we could have them for a meal and you could talk to both of them."

"Maybe, Granny. But I know Burnie wants to help so badly. I don't know if I should let him."

"He loves you, child. I can see that. Let him help as much as you are comfortable with. I am sure that if we ask Breck or Barnabas, they could find someone we could speak with."

"I know, Granny. I just feel awkward. I feel ashamed of how he beat me down so much." Muir was on her feet, running for her bedroom, the door closing quietly behind her.

Moira sighed, rising to walk where she could stand and watch Muir's door. Lord, I have no idea how to help her. How do I? She is hurting in so many ways. I guess it's good that she is. She losing the numbness and sense of loss that she had. I hate that she has lost her innocence though, Lord. I am sure that Stewart told her exactly what he had planned.

Burnie tapped at the door, and then peeked in, coming to stand beside Moira, an arm around her.

"Muir?"

"She's hurting, Burnie. She is starting to feel again, and is so ashamed of herself."

"I know, Granny. I know. I just wish I knew how to help her." Burnie frowned as he too stared at

Muir's door. "Moira, will you please bring her out here? If she will come? I need to talk to her."

"I will do what I can but I can't promise that she will."

They both looked up as Muir's door opened and she appeared in front of them, tears on her face as she reached to hug her grandmother.

"I'm sorry, Granny. I shouldn't have left you like that. It's not how you taught me."

"No, it isn't, Muir, but you are an adult. And you have been through so much." Moira held on her a lot longer, feeling Muir not wanting to let her go. "Your young man is here, Muir. He says that he needs to speak with you."

Muir looked over at Burnie. "He does?"

Burnie nodded, before he dropped to a knee, his hands coming out for Muir's. "Muir, you are a beautiful, sweet, compassionate lady who has been through so much. I love you, more than I thought I would ever love someone. Muir, I know that you are hurting and that you are healing. I would like to be the one who walks alongside you for the rest of your life." He paused, swallowing hard, his eyes on his lady love. "I do not want to put any pressure on you, sweetheart. I just wanted you to know how I feel and how I see you."

Muir blinked rapidly, trying to clear the tears from her eyes, and unable to. She finally struggled to free her hands, causing Burnie's heart to fall, as he thought that she had rejected him. He swallowed hard, his mouth opening to speak, watching as her hands covered her mouth. Muir was overcome for a moment, before she dropped to her own knees and threw herself into his arms, her own tight around his neck as sobs shook her body. Unable to speak, she simply nodded. Moira watched the young couple, saddened at how they had met but delighted that they were speaking of a future together. Bless them, Lord. They have a long ways to go, I understand that, but You are leading. I can see that.

Chapter 24

Breck watched Burnie the next morning as he ran for his car, not sure what was going on. He had been late coming home the night before and saw the lights still on in Burnie's office. He's going to wear himself out, he thought, before he shook his head, turning to find Muir standing near him.

"Muir? Looking for Burnie?" Breck grinned at her.

"No, actually, I'm not. I know he was heading into town. I wanted to talk with you for a moment, without Burnie around or without Granny hearing me." Muir looked troubled.

"Sure, let's head for the gardens." Breck didn't speak, instead watching Muir, trying to assess what she was thinking and unable to. "Here, this looks like a nice spot." Breck pointed to a wrought iron bench in the perennial gardens.

"Thank you, it does." Muir sat, her hands rubbing along her jeans, not sure how to begin to ask what she needed to.

"Muir? You were looking for me. For a reason, I know. Before we begin to talk, I want to pray with you. That's what I always do." Breck didn't wait for her to respond, instead bowing his head, his prayer full of verses about peace, about learning, about letting go, and then he prayed specifically for that for Muir. When he finished, he looked up to find her face wet with tears. "Muir?" He reached for his handkerchief, holding it out for her.

Muir took it, wiping at her eyes and face, and then twisting it in her hands. "I never had an older brother, someone who could teach me, or listen to me, or torment me, or just be my friend. Breck, you are that to me. You helped me when I needed help." She looked up at him. "Burnie talked to me last night. He told me that he loved me, that he wanted to walk alongside me for the rest of my life. I'm broken, Breck. How do I let him do that?"

Breck had suspected something like that. "I see. Burnie will have prayed and prayed hard about this. He may also have talked to Buckley, to get a pastor's perspective on what he would be facing, and what he should be doing. He has not rushed into this, not Burnie." He paused. "I know you are afraid for him. All the ladies were. Some suffered more than others, but God had provided for them. The couples each love each other more than anyone other than God."

Muir nodded. "I know. They've told me that. It's just that I feel like a failure. He's educated. I'm not. There is just so much uncertainty hanging over me right now, though."

"And Burnie will have considered that. Tell me, Muir. If you walked away from Burnie, how would you feel? Could you do that very thing?"

Muir shrugged. "It's just so new, Breck. I would walk away if it meant he survived. I know Stewart. He's evil and vindictive. He will go after Burnie for revenge. It won't matter if I'm around or not." She sighed, a hand rubbing at her forehead. "I just am so conflicted, I guess is what Granny would say. I don't want to ruin his life, but he sees something in me that no one other than Granny has seen in a long time. He makes me feels special and wanted and beautiful."

Breck smiled. "I think you have answered your question, Muir. If a man makes a lady feel like that, there is something there. I can't find the words to describe it, but it is how I would like my lady to feel, if I ever find her."

Sitting quietly, Muir mulled over Breck's words, knowing that just talking to him had helped her to sort through her thoughts. "Thank you, Breck. You have helped me. If Burnie and I do ever marry, can I ask a favour?"

"Sure, and it will happen, Muir. I see how he watches you. He won't let you escape him."

"I don't have someone to walk me to him. Would you?" When Breck didn't respond, Muir sighed, thinking that he would refuse. She looked up at him, finding him smiling at her.

"I would be honoured to, Muir. I would be honoured to." He gave her a quick hug and then prayed for her once more.

Muir finally rose, unable to speak, and almost ran for the building, leaving Breck standing and staring after her before he shook his head and moved on to where he had parked. He was needed at a meeting but for now, he didn't care that he was cutting it close to getting there. Muir had needed to talk with him and she came first today.

Chapter 25

Tucking the small box into his jacket pocket, Burnie left the jewelry store, pleased with his find. He walked back towards his car, his steps slowing as he neared it, watching the man leaning against it, before he shook his head.

"Murphy O'Brien! What brings you to town? And Ian Galbraith as well?" Burnie reached to shake their hands.

"You do. You and your lady." Murphy grinned. "Doing some shopping?"

Burnie laughed, his face lighting up as he thought of Muir. "I was. And no, I'm not showing you. Muir gets to see it first."

Ian grinned. "That's not fair, you know. When do we get to meet this lady?"

"Now, if you like. I'm heading home. Did you bring your ladies?"

"We didn't, not this time. Emma sent us and told us to talk to you and to Dallas." Murphy sobered as he spoke.

"I see. Unfortunately, Dallas is out of town today, up where Muir and Granny came from."

"Granny?" Ian and Murphy exchanged looks.

"Moira, Muir's grandmother. I call her Granny, just as Muir does." Burnie moved to the driver's side of his car. "I'll meet you there?"

"Burnie? Perhaps we should talk away from there first. I know you'll want to speak with Muir."

Burnie shook his head. "No. If it involves her, I want her in our discussion. I can't do it any other way. I'm sorry/"

"Don't apologize. Micah told us that would be what you said. He was right." Ian shrugged. "So, let's go find your lady."

Burnie watched the two men walk away before he pulled out his phone, finding no messages, but sending off a text to Muir, telling her that he loved her and would see her in a few moments.

Muir stared at the phone. "Did he really say that, Lord? Did he really tell me once more that he loves me?" She looked up as Imly and Locklin sat beside her.

"Muir? I know that look. Message from Burnie?" Imly just grinned at her.

"It was. He's special." Muir's face held a bemused look.

"He is, Muir. Very special." Locklin reached to hug her. "He has always made sure that we ladies are okay. The fellows all do."

"Thank you, Locklin. I never had that, you know. I am finding out how hard it was living in our village."

"It was difficult. Jaxcy had it hard for a few years, when she was on her own. Her town was really restrictive." Imly hesitated. "Muir, please don't take this wrong. But I do want to ask you something."

Muir shrugged. "Go ahead. Right now, everything just seems so mixed up."

"I understand." Imly reached to touch Muir's hair. "I would love to see you do something with your hair. I don't think it's you to have it so uneven."

"It's not." Muir blinked, not sure how to respond. "I loved my long hair and the curls and waves and ringlets. Stewart wanted it kept long. He kept touching it, telling me that I could never cut it. It was a hold he tried to have on me. One day, I just grabbed the scissors in the store and chopped it off. I kept doing that. He was so angry that he beat me. That was the first time that he did. I could hardly move for a few weeks, it was that bad. It didn't stop him from beating me again and again."

"To wear you down, I suspect, Muir." Locklin reached to touch her hair as well. "We would love to help you with it. If you like."

"I would like. I hate that it's like it is." Muir blinked as she stared down at the shoes in front of her. "Burnie? What are you doing here?"

"Looking for my sweetheart." He crouched down in front of her, his head tilted to watch her.

"Why?" Muir sighed. "I'm sorry. It hasn't been a good day."

"No, I suspect not. But these ladies here are waiting for you. I have a couple of friends as well who would like to meet you and speak with you."

Muir's eyes raised to where Murphy and Ian stood, their eyes on her.

"Who are they?"

"That's Murphy and Ian. They work for a friend's security team. They were sent here with some information for us."

Muir shrugged. "I guess. Which do I do first?"

"Whichever you want, Muir. I won't tell you that. You get to decide and we back you on your decision."

Muir stared at him before she spoke quietly. "I would like to go with Imly and Locklin, but I don't want to put the men out. Not if they have travelled to come here."

"It's okay, Muir. They understand. We can work away on what we need to. You just come and find us when you're ready to." He reached to kiss her forehead and then stood, watching for a moment before he walked away.

"Did he really just do that?"

"Do what?" Imly grinned at her.

"Walk away from me?"

"He did, Muir. He did. You made your decision, he's fine with it, and he'll find you later." Locklin stood. "Now, let's see how we can fix you up to make

---

119

you even more beautiful. Cadee had some more clothes for you, she said."

"She can't. Others need them."

"According to Cadee, these were given to her specifically for you."

Chapter 26

Two hours later, Muir approached the conference room, hesitation in her manner. She didn't see Imly following her, watching to see what she would do. Muir stopped, staring down at the new coloured jeans and the nice sweater that she was wearing, a multicoloured scarf tied around her neck, new leather loafers on her feet. Her hand touched her hair that Locklin had trimmed and shaped, telling Muir that it would grow long once more.

Muir finally stepped through the door, her eyes searching for Burnie, finding all the men but Breck and Barnabas there. She didn't see Burnie at first, and she frowned.

Benen looked up as the door closed, pausing for a moment before he turned to Burnie, who sat beside him.

"Burnie? Muir's here."

Burnie paused for a moment, his finger on the place he was reading.

"What was that?"

"Muir's here." Benen nodded towards the door. "I think she's looking for you and can't find you. She's ready to run."

Burnie shifted in his chair and then was on his feet, heading for Muir, finding her turning to him. He paused, a smile of delight lighting up his face.

"You are even more beautiful. What did they do?"

Muir gave a tentative smile. "Locklin trimmed my hair for me. Cadee gave me more clothes."

"They did? Just outward dressing on a very beautiful lady. Will I muss the outfit if I hug you?" He reached to do that as she gave a shy nod and then kissed her cheek. "I meant what I said. I love you." He reached for her hand. "Now, are you able to stay and talk to us? Or do the ladies have more plans for you?"

"I have time. Where do I need to sit?" Muir frowned at him for a moment. "Burnie?"

"It's okay, Muir. You have just taken my breath away. Here. Ian and Murphy are over at this table. Let me grab what I was working on and then we can speak with them."

Two hours later, Muir sat back, exhausted at the amount of material that she had just gone through. She was hurting, she thought, about what they had discovered and who had disappeared from her village. She had not realized that there had been so many over the years.

"Does Granny know?" Her voice was quiet. "She may but I don't know if she'll have put it all together." Muir was saddened. "Did he do that?"

"We suspect so." Murphy paused, watching her closely. "It's not your fault, Muir. You didn't cause him to do this or to hurt you or keep you locked up. It's the evil in him that did this. Emma is working on tracking down who he is working for and she has a good lead on that person. She'll forward what she finds to Dallas or Will."

Muir nodded. "I see. Burnie, I need to leave." She was on her feet, running from the room, leaving Burnie standing, staring after her before he too was gone.

Murphy and Ian exchanged looks, knowing well enough the emotions going through the couple, both of them having faced things with their ladies.

Barnabas dropped down into the chair Burnie had used and shifted through the papers.

"Finding who it is?"

"We are. Muir was gone before we could continue. Is she okay?" Ian was worried.

"No, I don't think that she is. She was held captive, as I am sure Burnie has told you, beaten and almost broken by this man." Barnabas' finger tapped Stewart's picture. "If Burnie hadn't been there, stepping in, and then the fellows bringing her here, she would not even still be in Canada."

"It was that close?" Murphy's face hardened.

"It was. We think that she was the only one to get away from him. That's driving him to plot revenge and try to extract it against both Burnie and Muir. Dallas, Breck and Andy are also on the radar as they're the ones who went up and brought them back."

Chapter 27

Catching up with Muir as she stopped in the lobby, Burnie just wrapped her into his arms, standing with his chin on the top of her head. He could feel the shudders running through her and grieved, knowing that part of what Muir was facing was grief as well.

"Sweetheart?" He finally spoke, before he directed her to a seat on the sofa in one of the sitting areas.

"Burnie? Why?"

"Greed. Money. Evil." Burnie sighed, not quite sure how to explain the darkness of a man's soul to a beautiful hurting lady.

"I get that. I just don't know how it happened in that village. We are less than one hundred in numbers."

"I know, sweetheart. I know. Evil doesn't look at numbers. Satan looks for someone he can use, and he found that in Stewart. From what Murphy and Ian said, Stewart was always like that. The people are starting to talk, now that his brother is no longer there. They were too afraid of retribution before."

"The ones who disappeared? Can we track them?"

"I'm not sure if we can. Emma and her team will give it a try, as will Dallas and his team and the provisional force will as well."

Muir sighed, her head going down on Burnie's shoulder, seeking comfort from him. "I hate this, Burnie, but if I hadn't been in that situation, God wouldn't have brought you to our village."

"Perhaps not, but you are the one that He meant for me. Of that I am confident." He grew silent, before he reached into his pocket. "I have something for you."

"You do? Everyone is always giving me something. I don't know what to give to the ladies in return."

"We'll come up with something, but I know for a fact that they don't want you to repay them. It's who they are. They model encouragement to others in their actions."

"That they do." Muir stared at the box in Burnie's hand. "What is that?"

Burnie grinned, before he lifted the lid from it with one hand, and then dropped the little velvet case from it. He paused, his eyes on Muir, a prayer raising in his heart. He had no idea what her answer would be.

"Muir, you are the one who completes my heart. I love you, more each hour and each day. I would like to be the one who walks alongside for as long as God allows us on this earth. Will you be my sweetheart for life? Will you marry me?" He opened the case to reveal a beautiful emerald ring.

Muir's hand covered her mouth and then tears sparkled in her eyes. "Burnie, even if I were to say no, your words have made be feel beautiful and loved and wanted." She looked up at him, to see the uncertainty that he was feeling on his face. "I will. I love you."

Burnie reached to kiss her and then slipped the ring on her finger, raising her hand to kiss it. "Thank you, sweetheart. I won't rush you into setting a date. You're healing and we need to let you do that."

Muir frowned at him, an adorable pucker between her brows. "What? Making me wait?" She snuggled down. "Thank you, Burnie. You have no idea how you make me feel."

"I think I do, to a certain extent." The couple grew quiet, content just to be together, not seeing the looks that were sent there way by the other members of the building family as they moved around the lobby.

Moira stood for a moment, her eyes on the two, before she turned to Murphy, who had tracked her down.

"Murphy? You said your team is heading for Ireland tonight?"

"We are, Moira. Emma is sending us. It's okay. We do that kind of stuff." He grinned at her. "She has found someone over there that we need to speak with. We'll be gone for a few days, but when we return, I'm brining my lady over to meet your granddaughter."

"Thank you, Murphy. I just wish I could find someone for her to speak with, even on a causal basis. She needs that."

"I have a friend whose wife is a retired forensics psychologist. She used to do a lot of profiling. She has been working with Emma on this. Darcie said that she would love to meet your Muir and talk with her."

"She did? Even without meeting her?"

"She did." Murphy looked around as Ian approached. "Listen, we have to run. You have our numbers. Call us for anything, even if you just need to talk. We'll be available."

Moira watched the men walk away before she turned back to her granddaughter and then approached the couple, sitting down beside Muir. Muir looked around at her grandmother, contentment on her face, before she reached out a hand.

"See, Granny? Burnie asked, I answered, and he's going to be part of our family. He's not leaving me."

"Did you really think that he would?" Moira touched her granddaughter's ring and then reached to hug the two, a prayer of blessing ringing in their ears. "Not rushing into it?"

"No, Granny, we're not. Muir needs this time to heal and to be absolutely sure of what she wants. That was taken from her. When we set a date, that will be her decision, or our decision as a couple." Burnie's eyes were on Muir as he spoke. "Muir?"

"I don't want to wait, Burnie, but I know that if we marry, it will make things a lot worse with Stewart." She closed her eyes as she drew a deep sigh. "Will I ever be free of him and his evilness?"

"Soon, child. Soon. Dallas called me earlier. He had tried to reach either you or Burnie but couldn't.

He's on his way back. Tomorrow is Sunday but he wants to meet with all of us, if he can."

"I'll speak with Breck. I'm sure that there will be no problem with most of us being there." Burnie sat back, content with the two ladies he now had in his life. Thank you, Lord, for Muir and Moira. I have a family now, all of my own, something that I never had.

Chapter 28

Dallas spoke with Burnie quietly before he moved to the front of the conference room, a heavy sigh coming from him as he dropped the folders that he had been carrying onto the table. This is not how I wanted to come today, Lord. I just don't know how much more Muir can take.

Barnabas studied his friend before he turned to Buckley who stood beside him, Locklin's hand tight in his.

"Buckley, we need your prayers right now. Lead us, please?"

Buckley did just that before he found his seat, his eyes on Burnie and Muir as they sat across from him, a prayer in his heart for his friends.

"Dallas? You have word?" Barnabas spoke from where he had taken a position leaning against a wall.

"I do. Thank you, Buckley. We needed your prayers." Dallas' eyes moved to Burnie and Muir. "Muir. Burnie. Moira. As you know, I was to your home village, Muir. I was working with the investigators who were brought in." He paused, once more, swallowing hard. "It was as you had suggested and suspected. We found the debris from the store in the ravine. We found human remains in that debris. But the cadaver dogs also made other hits."

Burnie's face grew stern. "More than one?"

Dallas nodded. "More than one. I am not at liberty to say how many but there were a number. The investigators now begin the gruesome task of identifying the remains and then following through to find their killers."

"Stewart." Muir's one word sounded as if it had been pulled from deep within her. "There will be others who aren't there. Where are they?"

"The investigation continues at his home, with the proper search warrants. Thanks to you, Muir, we have found the link that we were looking for in disappearances in the area of young men and women. I am sorry, though, that it had to be you."

"Where's Stewart?" Burnie had his eyes on Muir.

"We are actively looking for him, but have not found him. That's why we need you two to be as careful as you can for the next while. He will be coming after you both, that's a given."

"We know that, Dallas. We know that. But what else can you tell us?"

"At present, not a lot. Muir? Have you had any unwanted messages on your phone?" Dallas grinned at the look that she threw him.

"No. I thought you made sure I couldn't."

"We did that very thing, Muir." Dallas shook his head at her. "We just have to ensure that it doesn't happen."

"I've been getting them, Dallas, more and more brutal as each one comes. I've saved them to a file and sent them on to the lab."

"Thanks, Burnie. Now, I don't have much more information for you. I know you fellows are working away. Emma and her team are as well."

"What do they need to watch for?" Breck spoke from where he sat at the back of the room.

"The usual. Burnie, you've been through this with the others. Muir, stay close to someone at all times. Stay close to the building, although the building has been invaded at times. Keep your cells charged and on you at all times. Be aware of your surroundings where you are out and about." Dallas finally walked away, not satisfied with what he could share with the couple and Moira.

Quiet conversation broke out among the men and the ladies, Muir just sitting quietly, her eyes on the hands that she had folded on the tabletop. Moira watched her closely before she rose, turning to find Breck nearby.

"Breck? How do I keep Muir safe?"

"By doing what Dallas asked. That's what we do. It also helps to pray."

"I know that." Moira was frustrated, wanting this over for her granddaughter. "But how do we find this man and the ones over him?"

"That's what we're working on. I know that it's frustrating, Moira. It is for all of us. I can't tell you how to live, but please be as careful as you can. You are at risk as well. Stewart and whoever it is that employs him will not think twice to take you to get Muir to come out of hiding."

"I am aware of that. I have dealt with this man for years, Breck." Moira paused. "Let me think through the years and see what else I can discover for you."

Breck watched Moira walk away before he turned to find Branigan and Baird standing beside him.

"Fellows?"

"We've been talking, Breck, us and our ladies. I have a feeling the others have as well. What can we do to help Muir? The ladies are helping with her clothes and hair, but there is still more that we can do."

"Right at the moment? Pray. Be there for them both." Breck's eyes following Muir as she walked around the room, Berneen beside her. "Has she found someone to talk to?"

"Not that we know, but Burnie mentioned that Darcie was willing to speak with her." Baird watched his wife, Berneen.

"That's good. If it helps, we can arrange that." Breck pulled out his phone as it vibrated, frowning. "It's Abe. Sorry, fellows, I need to take this."

Breck walked away, answering Abe's call as he did so.

"Abe? You sound far away." Breck unlocked his office door and then sat behind his desk, reaching for a pen and paper out of habit.

"Breck? Are you somewhere you can speak freely?" Abe's voice held a tone that Breck could not place.

"I am. We just had a meeting with Dallas, but I'm in my office. Alone. What's going on?"

"Muir's parents? We found them."

Breck sat stunned, unsure that he had heard correctly. "What did you say, Abe? I thought you said you found Muir's parents."

"We have. That's why we came to Ireland. Emma found a clue, traced it, and we found them. We have them with us. We'll working with the authorities now, both here and at home. It will take a few days before we can head home, what with needing passports and whatnot, but we're be there."

Breck blinked rapidly, tears flooding his eyes. He swallowed hard. "I'll talk to Barnabas. How much do you want us to say?"

"At present, until we're on Canadian soil? Nothing to either Muir or Burnie. We're trying to keep it as quiet as we can. Pray for us."

"Done, my friend. And thank you." Breck set his phone down, wonder in his heart, a prayer of praise on his lips. Just like Jaxcy, Lord, just like Jaxcy. Her parents were alive. So are Muir's. Bless our ladies, dear Lord.

Chapter 29

Muir made her way the next morning towards Hagen's shop, Hagen's little girl in her arms, Hagen carrying her son. She looked around, interested for the first time, she thought, in the land that would become her home for real. She had stared hard at her emerald ring that morning, a prayer rising for Burnie, and then for herself. She felt unworthy to be the one that he had chosen but he had chosen her and that filled her with happiness, despite what she had faced and was still facing.

"We're near Lake Erie, Muir. Have Burnie take you down there sometime. It can be wild when the winds come up." Hagen nodded towards the distance, where Muir could see water.

"Is that what it is? I've stood and watched it, not knowing it was one of the lakes." She turned her face to the little girl, finding her staring at her before she grinned at Muir, a tooth peeking through her bottom gum.

"This is your shop, Hagen?" Muir stared around, amazed at the work. "These are wonderful."

"Thank you." Hagen placed her children into the playpen that she had set up near the desk. "We put in the wall here after I was attacked by the madmen who was after me. Come on through."

Muir finally stood back, her finger touching a small wooden puzzle. "These are amazing. I often would make things for myself, just to amuse myself, as

---

134

the children weren't friendly or weren't allowed to play with me."

"That's so sad." Hagen studied her before she reached for a paper and pen. "Talk to me, Muir. Tell me what you want to do. I could use some help in here if you are interested."

Muir's face lit up. "You can? But can you afford to pay me?"

Hagen began to laugh, causing Muir to frown. "I gather Burnie has not yet spoken to you? He should do, but each of us ladies receives wages through the Foundation, just as our husbands do. It's part of their mandate on encouraging couples."

"They do? It is? Oh, that's so wonderful. I thought I would be a burden on Burnie." Muir sank down onto a stool.

"Never a burden, Muir. Not with Burnie. He would never think that." Hagen was off then, describing her work, what she had done, what her goals were, and how she just knew that Muir would be an asset to her. "Have you had any training in art?"

"No, but my father was an artist on the side. He wanted to establish himself but never got a chance to do that. Granny says that I follow in his footsteps, with my drawings and little crafts that I did." She frowned. "Stewart took that away from me."

"Not any longer. Here. Draw me something. A new toy that you don't see here, that would work for children ages three to five." Hagen walked away, talking to her children, and then reaching for the computer, drawing up her website and then printing off the orders. The business was growing, she thought, thank you, Lord. It is reaching out to be the blessing that I want it to be. She turned as she heard Muir approaching her.

"What's that?" Muir pointed to the computer monitor.

"My website." Hagen was off the chair, pushing Muir down. "Here. Use the mouse and work your way around it." She reached for the paper that Muir still held and drew in her breath. "Muir? You are a true artist. I like this. It's whimsical but so like a little fox. What made you do that?"

Muir shrugged, not really listening to her. "I guess I used to watch them at home. They fascinate me." She pointed to a section on the website. "What's this?"

"That? A friend is providing photos with verses to go along with the toys. It's another avenue to reach out and witness."

"I like that. Do you do cards and stationery as well?"

"No, but we could expand. Muir, I think you just found what you want to do. You can take her photos and design the cards. A printer in town already works with me. He would do the cards and stationery as well."

"He would? Oh, then, okay. Let me think it through and pray about it."

"And talk to Burnie."

"Oh, no! He won't want me doing this." Distressed, Muir sat back, not having heard the door open and Burnie and Brandon approach, the children squealing with glee as they saw their father.

"I wouldn't want you to do what?" Muir jumped as Burnie crouched down beside her, an arm around her.

"This. These photos. Hagen has suggested that I design cards and stationery using photos." Muir bit at her lip with uncertainty.

"I think it's a wonderful idea. Working like this, with Hagen? You two suit each other as friends. I know Hagen has wanted to expand, but is busy enough or almost too busy already with her tools." Burnie grinned at Hagen.

"You do? You wouldn't mind?" Muir turned to him, wonder in her heart that he would even consider letting her do that.

"I do. I am not going to step in and tell you no, not if it's what you really want to do. You're free here, Muir. You can make your own decisions. I just ask that you talk to me when you do. When we marry, then we discuss whatever it is as a couple, pray about it and make a decision together."

"I see. Granny told me that was how it should be. I didn't have a married couple that I could watch or follow, not with Mom and Dad gone."

"We understand that, sweetheart. Any of the ladies here will talk with you. Buckley will advise you as a pastor. I know that he's no longer the pastor of our church, but he is still our pastor as well as a friend. Anything you discuss with him, stays with him, unless you give permission for him to talk to someone. And that someone is usually just Locklin."

Chapter 30

Stewart Holman stood in the shadows of the trees, his gaze fixed on the door to Hagen's shop. He had watched as the two women had entered and then the two men. His anger burned inside him. He would deal with that man, get him out of the way, and then deal with Muir. It was too late now for him to receive the money that had been promised, the buyer moving on to someone else. She had cost him millions, he thought, and she would pay with her life. Stewart really didn't care how she died, just that she did.

He turned and made his way from the forest to the road where he had left his vehicle, a high-end vehicle at that, one that stood out on the gravel road. He didn't know that he had been spotted by a neighbour to the Foundation family, and that his license plate and vehicle description had already made its way to the police department. He drove off, the patrol vehicle just missing him.

Muir shuddered with sudden fear as she and Burnie walked back towards the building they called home, her hand tight in his. She eyes the woods with anxiety and sudden knowledge that Stewart had been around, but she could not prove it. She just knew how she felt when he was.

Burnie watched her closely before his eyes too sought the woods. It had been used before to harm the ladies and men who he called friends. He picked up his pace, walking more rapidly towards the building and inside, stopping for a moment to glance out the windows.

"Is Granny around today?" His question brought Muir's attention back to him.

"She should be. We can go find her." Muir started to move away but stood still as Burnie tugged at her hand.

"Are you sure about the design work?"

"I am. I would like to try it. I told Hagen that my father was hoping to establish himself as an artist." She turned to look out the window. "Stewart was out there."

"He was?" Burnie reached to hug her. "I'm sure that he was. Dallas said he was in the area. I have no doubt that he knows exactly where you are."

"But I don't want him to hurt anyone." Muir was growing agitated.

Burnie hugged her tighter and then bent his head and began to pray for her. He felt her relax against him. When he was finished, he raised his head, searching her face and then bent and kissed her.

Muir stared up at him, wonder on her face, her fingers touching her lips. She finally moved away from him before turning and coming back into his arms, welcoming his second kiss.

"Muir?"

"Burnie?" She leaned back to stare up at him. "You told me that it was my decision. I fear for you, that Stewart will harm or kill you, but I have peace about us. God has been working in my life. That much I know. My decision? That we wed and now. I don't know how long we will have. Only God knows that."

Burnie just smiled and kissed her again, then turned her towards the stairs, her hand tight in his. "We need to find Granny. Do you know how long I have waited to have a grandmother? All my life."

Moira took one look at the young couple and then swept them into a hug, her prayer of blessing on them. She stood back, a hand on each of their arms.

"You have made a decision." Her statement was just that, a statement of fact and not a question.

"We have, Granny." Burnie's eyes were on Muir. "I told Muir that the timing of our wedding would be her decision. She has made that. We want to marry now, not wait until this is all resolved."

"Somehow, that's what I thought you would say." Moira turned to her granddaughter, seeing the flush of first love on her face. "Muir, I wish that your parents were here today, to walk with you through this exciting time in your life. But they aren't. I have something that I did manage to bring with me when the man helped me to escape. Michael gladly brought the box for me." She pointed towards Muir's bedroom. "Your mother's wedding dress is on your bed. I kept it for you."

Muir's tears blinded her for a moment, as she realized that she would have part of her family with her that day. She reached for her grandmother, holding on tight, before she spun back to Burnie's arm.

"Now what, Burnie?"

He grinned down at her. "Now what? I need your identification to get the application for the wedding license and then I can do that. We need to speak with Buckley, if you want him to marry us."

Muir nodded. "And here in the chapel? Can we do that?"

"We can and shall." Burnie swooped in for another kiss, dropped a kiss on Moira's cheek and then was off, running for his car and then heading for town.

"Granny? Did I just do something I might regret?" Muir was troubled.

"No, you didn't. It has been prayed over by all of us, and if you have peace, then you know you have made the right decision. Burnie has been teaching you to trust and pray, has he not?"

"He has, Granny. He has taken the lead in our relationship in that, just like you taught me."

"Then, let's move on to what we need to do. When are you thinking?"

"Tomorrow night? If everyone is around that is." Muir was troubled again for a moment before she pulled out her phone. "I can check without going door to door, can't I? Oh, this phone is so wonderful. Now to figure out how to do a group text. There. Did it." She spun as she heard a tap at the door, stepping back as the ladies of the building, including Anna and Amy and Hagen's twin sisters, bustled in, ready to help plan her wedding.

Chapter 31

Stewart stared at the newspaper two days later, frustration in his demeanour. She had to do that, now didn't she? She had to marry and move on. I won't let her. He crumpled the paper and tossed it into a trash can, stopping as he saw a man standing in his way.

"Out of my way! I want by." Stewart went to move around him, but felt instead his wrists caught behind him and the feel of steel on them even as he heard the snap of the handcuffs.

"I don't think so." Dallas stared him down. "We've been watching you, Holman. For starters, you are under arrest for kidnapping, forcible confinement, assault. We'll be adding murder to that. Read him his rights." Dallas turned away, his stomach roiling at the memory of what he had seen when he had been in Muir's village.

Pulling out his phone, he stared down at it, listening to the protests that Stewart was making. Dallas shook his head and moved away, dialling Burnie's number.

"Burnie? It's Dallas. Call me when you get this." Frustrated at only receiving Burnie's voice mail, Dallas reached for his keys, knowing that he needed to be across town at another crime scene. This is wearing me out, he thought. I need a break and just can't catch one.

Burnie frowned as he listened to Dallas' message, and then shrugged, setting his phone to one side and reaching instead for his Bible. He could hear Muir as she moved around the apartment, just getting to know it, she said. He smiled. She was just who he needed, he thought. Thirty minutes later, he reached for his phone again, this time leaving a message for Dallas. This is what is going to happen, he thought. Phone tag.

Muir hesitated in the doorway, her eyes on him. Burnie rose, a smile on his face, and went towards her, sweeping her into a hug and then kissing her. He stood back to watch her face, keeping his arms around her.

"Muir?"

"Dallas called. He said that he had been trying to reach you."

"He had. He left a voice mail that I finally had a chance to return. What did he want?"

Muir chewed at her lip for a moment. "He arrested Stewart this morning."

"He did? In town?"

Nodding her head, Muir snuggled closer to him. "In town. But he's sure that Stewart is not here on his own."

"No, he wouldn't be. He'll need to go through the courts now for the charges and then make bail if he can."

"I think he will. Whoever is behind him will not want him talking."

They turned to walk back towards the kitchen, and then to the entry door. Moira stood there, her hand raised to knock.

"I didn't get a chance to knock." She smiled at the couple. "Apparently, I am to bring you two down to the conference room. The other conference room."

"You are?" Burnie grinned as he kissed her cheek. "Then, if you must, you must. Muir, I can almost guarantee that there's a meal set out in there."

"There is? Why?"

"Because we refused on on Thursday night, when we married. They'd have made plans for today. Everyone is around."

Dallas stood for a moment, watching the couple, before he turned to Barnabas, motioning towards the hallway.

"What's up, Dallas? You're not happy." Barnabas paced beside him.

"I'm not. Holman has confessed to being out here. We know that's not on his own. I just wanted to give you a heads' up and let you work your wonders, if you can, with your security people."

"Thanks. We found evidence of someone or more than someone around. Near the gym in fact. It doesn't surprise me." He turned back towards the conference room, heading for the door. "You're staying."

"I wish I could. I have too many investigations on the go. I'll be back." Dallas walked away, fatigue in his body weighing him down.

Barnabas shook his head, opening the door to find Breck heading his way, pointing behind him.

"Abe called. He's heading for here."

"He is? Did he say why?"

"He did. He has news for Moira and Muir."

Barnabas froze and then nodded. "He was over in Ireland, now wasn't he?"

"He was. I'm heading up to make sure the suite beside Moira is ready. He asked that we not say anything, not until he lands here and is in front of them."

Chapter 32

Her eyes on Burnie as they finally stood, alone again, in the rose garden, she just reached to hug him. Thank you, Lord. You are healing me, teaching me how to live again. She frowned as Burnie's hand reached to touch her face and then he kissed her. His arms around her, he hugged her to him.

"Have I told you today that I love you?"

"You have. I love you too. Did you see Dallas?"

Burnie shook his head. "Was he here?"

"He was, but he left quickly. He's burning out, as you would say, Burnie. He's doing too much." She looked up again at him, finding him staring past her. "Burnie?"

"Muir? Can you turn around for a moment?"

"I can, if I have to."

"I think that you need to. Abe, Ian and Murphy are here. They're looking for us."

Muir turned, her eyes on the men before she saw movement behind them. Her head tilting, she broke free from Burnie's hug and walked towards Abe, looking past him. She looked up at him, seeing the smile on his face and then his nod. Muir moved past him, Burnie reaching for her hand and walking with her.

Burnie stopped short of the couple who stood there, his eyes flickering between Muir and the lady.

He waited for Muir, finding her struggling to free her hand from his, her hands then covering her mouth.

"It's you! I dreamed about you last night. That you were here." She moved to stand directly in front of the lady who looked so much like her. "Are you my mother? And my father?"

"We are, Muir." The man hesitated before he reached out a shaking hand, to lay it against her curls. "You are alive. We were never sure."

"And I was told you were dead. So was Granny." She drew back, wonder on her face. "Does Granny know?"

"Not yet." Abe spoke from behind her, even as his team of seven tall men surrounded them. "How be we head inside?"

"We can do that." Burnie reached for Muir's hand, finding her reluctant to move. "Muir? Sweetheart? We need to move inside."

"Oh, we do? I'm sorry." She turned and walked with him, glancing frequently over her shoulder. "Did you know?"

"No, I didn't. I'm so happy for you, Muir, and for Granny." He stopped just inside the lobby door, watching as Moria walked their way.

Moira came to a sudden halt, her eyes on Muir and Burnie and then drifting past them, to stop on the other couple.

"Morgan? Oh, Morgan, is that you?" She was across the room, in her son's arms as they both wept before she freed herself to turn to Muir's mother.

"McRae? You as well? Oh, the Lord has answered my prayers." Both ladies wept as they stood, arms tight around one another. "How?"

"That's what we'll explain." Abe spoke from beside them, looking around, uncomfortable at being in the open, even though they were inside. "Can we move to a room?"

"Certainly. How about the chapel?" Breck pointed that way.

The men and ladies from the building filed into the back seats, leaving the front for Muir and Burnie and her family. Abe paced at the front, suddenly at a loss for words. He looked at Murphy, who simply grinned and nodded.

"Abe? How?" Burnie finally spoke.

"It's a long story, and we don't have it all yet. Morgan and McRae have been working with the authorities on both sides of the Atlantic to give their statements. There is still a lot of work to be done." Abe nodded towards where Muir sat, her parents on either side of her. "They have quite the story."

"Holman?"

"Holman. According to what they have said, he has had his eye on Muir since she was a baby. That's immoral and heartbreaking."

"He separated them because of that?"

Abe nodded. "That's what they were told. He was afraid that if they stayed, they would move away. Have you seen her baby pictures?"

"No, but I am sure that she was a very pretty baby."

"She was. When we walked into the house where they were kept captive, all Morgan asked was if Muir was okay. That has driven them all these years. He did say that they were very close to escaping when we walked in. They had been able to reach out to someone in the government."

"I am glad to hear that, but it doesn't change the fact that a baby was without her parents all of her life."

"No, it doesn't." Abe looked around. "Listen, we have to run. Emma and I will be back in a couple of days. She wants to talk with Muir and her family as well as you, Burnie. Do you want Doug and Darcie to come as well?"

"I think so. Maybe Darcie can give us some more light."

Abe grinned. "Check your email. Emma passed your email address on to Darcie, who was sending you information."

"Okay. I haven't seen it but I'll check my spam folder. I've been trying to work through some revisions."

"I'm sure you have." Abe suddenly laughed. "Did a mystery writer ever expect to become involved in his own mystery?" With that, he walked towards Muir and her family and then out of the chapel, his men filing out after him.

Chapter 33

Muir wandered their apartment that night, troubled that she had been the reason that her parents had been taken out of her life. She had always thought that it had been business that had done that. Burnie stood and watched from his office doorway before he approached her and wrapped her into his arms, finally sweeping her up and then finding his favourite chair, just holding her as she wept, his own tears dampening her hair.

She was finally still, her emotions spent, but there was still a turmoil inside her. Burnie knew that and prayed for her. He finally felt her relax as she slept. He refused to move, just shifting to a more comfortable position. He heard his phone ringing from the office and ignored it. Right now, Burnie decided that Muir needed him. His head went down and he slept.

Muir roused hours later, surprised to find herself wrapped in Burnie's arm as he slept in his chair. She slipped away, squinting at the clock. Five in the morning, she thought. Burnie is usually up soon. Muir paused in the kitchen, finally deciding to shower and change her clothes. She didn't know what the day would bring, but she felt refreshed in her heart, knowing that her parents were still alive and right here, in the building. She searched for her phone, smiling as she found Abe's phone number programmed into it. She sent off a short text to thank him and then headed for the kitchen, finding Burnie already there, her tea ready for her and on the table, his mug of coffee there as well.

Burnie turned as he heard Muir and simply opened his arms, catching her as she threw herself at him, her arms around his neck as she hugged him tight.

"Did yesterday really happen?"

He nodded. "It did. Your parents are here, in the apartment next to us for now. Barnabas will let them decide where they want to be. But for now, he'll keep them here, until we can find the ones responsible."

"I am still in shock. God knew all along, didn't He?" At Burnie's nod against her head, she hugged him tighter. "This is what you mean, isn't it? What you're trying to teach me about God? That He knows our path and has plotted it out for us?"

"It is, sweetheart. It's been hard for you. I can't begin to imagine how your parents have felt, knowing that you were in his sights, and not knowing if you would escape him. Abe sent me a text last night. He had a chance to speak with them, telling them what had happened to you and how you and Granny escaped."

"Granny! How is she taking this?" Muir leaned back to look up at him.

"She's taking it just fine, she tells me. I talked to her a bit ago. She's planning on coming breakfast in about twenty minutes." Burnie squinted at the clock. "That will give me a chance to shower, shave and change. That is, if a certain bride will let go of me." He grinned at her look of pretended outrage before he kissed her thoroughly and then headed away to do just that.

Muir stared at the doorway, before she shook her head, a smile on her face, and headed for the fridge and then the pantry, not sure what to make for breakfast, or even if there were would be more than three of them. She looked back at the doorway and then headed for the entry, to tap at the door where her parents were. Morgan stood for a moment, staring at his daughter, all grown up and married now, and felt the sadness and yes, anger in him.

"Dad?" Muir sounded hesitant. "Have you and Mom eaten yet? I know there's a time change."

"We had some toast earlier, child. Come in."

"Oh, I wanted to ask you two for breakfast. We're just getting up." She stepped backwards, ready to head away when Morgan spoke.

"It wouldn't matter, child. We will come with you. Even if it's only tea that we have, we want to be there. We need to get to know you and your young man." McRae had appeared beside him as he spoke.

"Oh, okay. Come over when you're ready."

"We'll come now, if we may." McRae searched her daughter's face, finally reaching to hug her, missing all the years of just being able to do that.

Burnie looked around as he heard their voices and then reached to hug them. I like this, he thought. All the hugs that I missed as a child, I'm getting now. Moira stood beside him, an arm wrapped around him.

"They're hurting, Burnie."

"I know. So are you and Muir. We'll need to find someone for you all to talk with."

"I've been talking with my Lord, but I know what you mean. That Abe said he had a friend he would send our way."

"Darcie. I hope her husband, Doug, comes as well. He's a lieutenant on their Emergency Task Force in his hometown. They may have insight that we don't."

Chapter 34

Breck was on a hunt. He needed to speak with Burnie, and just couldn't find him. His car was in the parking lot. He sighed, as he stood outside, his hand rubbing at the back of his neck. He could feel eyes watching him, waiting for what, he wasn't quite sure.

"Bradon? Have you seen Burnie?" Breck called to Bradon as he walked by with Kade.

"Burnie? I think he was heading for Hagen's shop. Muir was there with her parents."

"Okay, thanks. The one place where I didn't look." Breck headed that way, his steps slowly as he neared the woods. We need to clear that back, he thought. It's getting too close to the building. A nice playground here for the little ones would be just the thing. I know Hagen would like it.

Popping open the door to the shop, he listened, smiling as he heard Burnie's voice teasing Hagen and then Muir, Hagen responding in kind. He stood for a moment in the doorway to the shop itself, watching as Morgan and McRae wandered the area, stopping examine the toys and puzzles.

Burnie looked around, and then excused himself, heading towards Breck, who backed away into the reception area.

"Breck? You're here for a reason?" Burnie pulled the door closed behind him.

155

"I am. Abe called. He didn't call you, not knowing if Muir would be around. He's had word that someone is in the area, looking for her."

"Holman?"

"He's still in jail. Hasn't made his bail, Dallas tells me. No, it's someone related to him. Abe didn't have all the specifics. Dallas also called. They're getting word on the street that someone has put a hit out on you."

"That's par for the course." Burnie frowned, his eyes on the floor. "So, what do we do? We can't stop living. I won't ask that of Muir."

"I know. We don't expect you to. We need to up our security around you. I talked to the security head. His people are moving in around you two. You go nowhere without one of them."

Burnie sighed, and then nodded. "We knew this would happen. Muir and I talked about it. The thing of it is, she doesn't want security. She wants whoever it is to come after her."

"She what?" Breck stared at Burnie. "That's exactly what we don't want."

Shaking his head, Burnie held up a hand to stop Breck's words. "Think about it from her perspective. She was confined for how long? Beaten? Threatened? Demeaned? Broken? She doesn't want to live like that again, to feel like she is a prisoner. She knows that's not what this means, but she still has that hesitation or fear, I guess you could say."

"I understand that, Burnie, but how do we do it then? We can't have them coming after you, if we can help it. You might not survive."

"We've talked about that too, Breck. Since we married and she feels safe with me, she's opening up and talking. A lot. Some things we will need to reach out to Dallas with. Other things? That's between her and I. I will not break her confidence in those."

Breck nodded. "Okay. Just talk to her? Please? She's part of our family, and you know that we take care of our own." Breck paced. "How is it going with her parents?"

"That? It's difficult. They're strangers yet related. It's going to take a long time. Muir may never fully accept them. She and Granny are a pair who have faced what life has thrown at them together. There's a bond there that she will not break. To have Morgan and McRae here? She feels threatened by them. I won't tell them that. They need to work that out."

Breck nodded. "Is Darcie heading this way?"

"Doug called and said they were. Hoping to make it today or tomorrow. I promised them a suite for the night if they wanted it. Doug seemed to think that they would."

"Sure. The guest suite on the first floor is available. We'll need to make arrangement for Morgan and McRae for wherever it is that they want to live."

"I know. For now, let it lie. I spoke with them briefly. Morgan knows how hard it is for all of them.

He seemed to think that at some point they would need to put some space between them."

"I see. Okay, then. I'll need to speak with him, then. Dallas said he's on his way out later as is Will."

"Good. Dallas needs to talk to them. I worry about them now that they're here. I also worry about my bride. This is the point in my novel when things heat up. I don't want to see that for Muir."

"And it will, Burnie. The fellows all want you to know that they're starting to pull in from their work, heading to the conference room every day. And Phil called. He said not to worry about your volunteer work with the driving school. He'll look after it for now."

"He did? I had a text from him that I haven't had a chance to answer today. I'll call him."

Burnie watched as Breck walked away and then left the building himself, to stand and stare towards the lake before he walked around the building, his eyes on the trees and underbrush near it. Like Breck, he became concerned.

Chapter 35

Muir looked around the gardens later that afternoon, feeling scared suddenly and then turning and running for the building. She had just needed to be outside for a bit, on her own. She knew the security guard had followed her but had stayed back to let her have space.

"Muir?" The guard was beside her, a hand on her back as she stopped suddenly, staring back the way that she had just ran from.

"I'm sorry. All of a sudden I felt scared and alone. I shouldn't have come out."

"No, it's okay. I was watching you. I just couldn't figure out what happened. In you go. I'll go back and see what it was." He looked up as Brendon and Brennen approached. "Fellows, can one of you stay with Muir and the other come with me?"

Brendon nodded, heading inside with Muir, as Brennen walked beside the guard.

"What happened, Paul?"

"Muir was frightened. I was watching and didn't see anything. I told her I'd have a look around."

Brennen finally stopped, staring at the ground. "She was right. With the rain last night, this is muddy. Someone has been here and here for a while. The footprints are too trampled on from him moving around."

Paul nodded and then looked through the trees. "The animal path. That's how they're getting in here."

"They are. We can't block it off." Brennen turned back to study the building. "She can't be caged."

"No, she can't. Not after what she went through." Barnabas had had a brief talk with all the security guards, giving a short history of what Muir had faced. Paul remembered the anger that had flooded through the whole group. "We want to help her stay safe."

"We know you do. We'll need to talk to Burnie."

"That we will." Paul hesitated and then pointed. "What's that?"

Brennen turned back, his eyes following the direction that Paul was pointing in. "An envelope. What do you want to bet it's a threat?"

"That would be my guess."

Brennen pulled out his handkerchief and picked up the envelope. "It's thick. They must have put in more than one threat."

Burnie turned from his computer monitor as he heard Brennen's voice.

"Brennen? What are you doing here? I thought you and Brendon were off somewhere."

"We were. We met Paul and Muir coming back in. Muir had been to the gardens and was scared. Paul and I searched around, found this." Brennen handed over the envelope. "We found a spot where someone had been waiting, but the tracks are too muddled now to try and figure them out. It looks as if whoever it was used the animal path."

"The animal path? Of course, that's perfect for them getting in and out." Burnie laid the envelope down and then reached for his phone, pulling up the camera app. "Here, take pictures as I open it."

"Are you sure that you should?"

"I am. I send the photos on to Dallas or the lab. This has gone on far enough. I want it to end."

"I know you do. Okay, I'm set."

Brennen began to take the pictures as Burnie turned the envelope over and over and then reached for his letter opener to slit the envelope. Burnie paused, a prayer raising, before he pulled out the papers inside.

"There are a lot. More than what I would expect if it was just a threat." He looked up at Brennen.

"That's what Paul and I thought. Okay, go for it, Burnie. Let's see what's there."

Burnie unfolded the papers, and counted them. "There are twelve of them, Brennen. He pulled back the last one. "This one has a signature and a date. What is this?"

"I have no idea. Sounds like a confession or something."

"Or something, is right." Burnie began to read, finally sitting down, setting each page where Brennen could take a picture of it. He finally looked up, finding Brennen staring at him in shock.

"Is that a confession?"

"It seems that way. He has named a lot of people that I would never have thought of. Wait! Ker's mother is named in here." Burnie sat back abruptly. "She was involved in this?"

"Oh, man! That sucks. Now we have to talk to Brody and Ker as well."

"That we do." Burnie looked past Brennen as the door opened and Dallas peeked in before he entered. "Just the man that we need to see."

"I am? Why?"

Burnie pointed to his desk. "Take a look at this. It's a confession from someone. And he names Kelly."

"Kelly? Ker's mother? Involved with Muir?" Dallas frowned as he reached for the papers and read through them. "I need a copy of these." He rose and headed for the copier, making copies and then returning the original to the envelope. He reached into his pocket for an evidence bag. "I need to take this."

"We know that. Now, how do we proceed? I can't hide this from Muir or from Brody and Ker."

"No, we can't. Burnie, go find Muir. Brody and Ker were around. I saw them as I came in." Dallas rose, following Burnie from the room.

Muir, Ker and Brody stared at the three men before they took the copies of the papers that they were being handed.

"Burnie?" Brody's voice had a stern tone to it.

"Read through them. Then we talk."

———

Chapter 36

Muir looked up as she heard a strangled sob from Ker, not understanding what was wrong. Brody simply wrapped Ker into his arms, their papers falling to the floor. Turning to Burnie, Muir was surprised at the sadness on his face.

"Burnie?"

"Ker's mother was involved in helping people who made teens and young children disappear. She was killed during the investigation. Ker was at risk." Burnie wrapped Muir in his arms. "That's the Kelly who is mentioned."

"Oh, Ker! How sad!" Muir moved to hug Ker. "I'm sorry. I didn't know."

"Nor did I. Keafe and I didn't know until Brody became involved in it all."

"Oh!" Muir turned back to Burnie, finding Brennen and Dallas watching her closely. "This person who signed this? He is a cousin of the Holmans. He wasn't around a lot. In fact, I hadn't seen him for the last six or seven months I was there." She sighed. "About the time Granny disappeared. Did he follow her?"

"We don't know. And somehow I don't think that we'll find him to verify this statement." Dallas looked down at it. "He has had it notarized, which tells me that he wrote in out in the presence of a lawyer, likely. Where he is now is anyone's guess."

"He was the one who was here today. Wasn't he?" Muir looked up at Brennen.

"More than likely, Muir. We found evidence that he had been waiting for a while. Dallas, I'll show you where. There is an animal path that he could follow."

Dallas had left with Brennen, returning shortly, a stern look on his face. He nodded at Burnie and Brody before he looked back down at the evidence bag. For once, he wasn't sure what to do. Normally, he had no trouble with that.

"Dallas?" Muir's voice brought his head back up. "We need to talk to Mom and Dad. You need to, I should say. I can't. I don't know them well enough to say anything."

"I will, Muir. I understand that they are in town with Barnabas and Amy at the moment. I'll track them down." He stayed for a few more moments and then left.

Brody watched the door close before he spoke. "Burnie?"

"I know, Brody. I know. It now involves you and Ker. And Keafe. Ker, where's Keafe?"

"I have no idea. I have not heard from him in a month. He said that he was taking off and would be in touch. I didn't expect it to be this long. He's not answering his phone. I've been sending texts and leaving voice mail."

"Let Dallas deal with that, then." Burnie sank back into his chair. "We need to start looking into this, but right at the moment? I hav an email that I have to answer. Muir? Please?" He reached for her hand even as Brody and Ker said their goodbyes and left.

"Burnie?"

"Muir, how good are you at proofreading?"

"I was top of my class in English. I always enjoyed it. Why?"

"Because I could use your help. It will help distract you from what's going on." He pointed to a binder. "In that is my latest work. Would you consider it?"

"Do you have to ask?" She eagerly reached for it. "Of course, I will. Can I work here? And what do I use to mark it up?"

"Mark it up, is it?" Burnie grinned at her as he stood and swooped in to kiss her. "Hmm. I think I could handle having you working with me."

"Listen, fellow. You just hired me. No kissing the staff." She smirked at him as she reached for a highlighter and pen and then settled herself down in an easy chair, soon immersed in the story.

Burnie watched her, content for her to be with him. That way, he thought, I can keep an eye on her. Lord, protect my bride. Keep her safe. Lead to a resolution of this and soon. I love to see how she is opening up to You and asking questions that drive me back into the Word, to find the answers that she needs.

Burnie finally stood, his work done for the day, to find Muir still engrossed in the story. He reached to gently shut it, bringing a protest from her.

"I am at the most interesting point, Burnie." She reached for the binder, finding him holding up and away from her, a grin on his face.

"It's supper time, Muir. I'll give it back. I promise. How be we call it a day for now?"

"Only if you bring that with you." Muir stood and stretched, keeping the highlighter and pen in her hand. "These go with me."

Chapter 38

Burnie ran for the rose garden the next morning, knowing that Muir had headed that way. Dallas had called, sounding rushed, and warning Burnie that Stewart had escaped from custody as he was being transferred to another city. They had word that he was heading their way.

Sliding to a halt, Burnie watched as Muir stood, her hand on a rose, before he approached her.

"Burnie?" She looked up, her smile lighting her face. "I didn't know you were here."

"I just got here. That's a beautiful rose. You can pick it."

"No, I don't think so. God is such a wonderful creator. I don't know how someone can look at flowers or nature and not see His hand in it."

"I don't either." Burnie's arm was around her, turning her back towards the building. "What are you up to now?"

"I had hoped to find Hagen, but she said that she had to head for town. Something about needing more material. I'm at a loose ends. Mom and Dad are away again, this time with the police. Granny is off with Anna."

"Then, let's find something fun to do. I don't have to work right now, I'm between books. The proofreading that you did has helped." He walked them to the building. "How about running away for the day?"

"We can do that?"

"We can. Let's head into town. I'll take you out for lunch and then window shopping."

"Window shopping? I've never done that. But what do we do with the windows when we buy them?" She smirked as Burnie stared at her before he broke out into gales of laughter.

"Got me there, sweetheart."

Three hours later, Muir pulled Burnie into a little shop, her mouth rounding as she stared at the treasures there. It was a little gift shop, full of unique gifts, mostly of glass. She wandered the store, listening to Burnie as he talked to the owner, a lady from the church. He finally moved to stand beside her as she stood, her finger lightly tracing a hand-blown rainbow.

"This is what I feel like right now, Burnie. That God saw me and promised me His rainbow." She looked up as he didn't speak, finding his eyes on it.

Burnie reached for it. "Then, you'll take it with you. You need these visual reminders as well as the ones that you find in Scripture." He nodded towards the store. "Find anything else?"

She shook her head, her eyes still on his. "No, just that. Are you sure, Burnie?"

"I am sure." He covered the price tag, before she could protest. "The cost doesn't matter, sweetheart. What matters is what it means to you. Evelyn?"

Evelyn shook her head as Burnie tried to pay. "No, it's a gift to Muir. I know that she's been struggling. No, Muir. No one but God has told me that. I can see the peace of His that you are finding. God bless you, dear." Evelyn watched them walk away before she wiped at her eyes and then dug into her purse to pay for the rainbow.

Muir set the rainbow carefully on the mantle when they got home, her finger once more tracing the colours on it. God, You have provided hope and a promise in Your rainbow. I need that. Burnie is part of the hope I have. Thank you, dear Lord.

Burnie had watched Muir before he stepped from the apartment, tapping on Moira's door. When she answered, he simply hugged her and then guided her back to his own apartment.

Moira watched Muir before she reached to hug her granddaughter.

"Found your rainbow?"

"I did, Granny. The lady in the shop wouldn't take anything for it, said it was a gift. That's what God does, isn't it? Gives us gifts when we least expect it."

"He does just that, child. He delights in surprising us. You always liked your rainbows, calling them pretty when you were tiny. Burnie, thank you for finding it for her."

Burnie shrugged. "Muir needed to do something fun for a change, something that she had never done. She wanted to buy the windows though when we were window shopping." He grinned at Muir as she sputtered before she began laughing.

"He wanted to take me window shopping, Granny. What was I supposed to think?"

Moira laughed, liking the lightness of spirit she was seeing in Muir, but knowing that the darkness still hung over the couple.

"Have you talked to Dallas today, Burnie?" Moira turned to find him heading for the kitchen.

"No, I haven't. I didn't expect to. He's off for a few days. Will made him take some time."

"Oh! The poor man. He's wearing out. He won't be on the force much longer. He's needing to find what he's searching for."

"He has been through a lot. He's become a good friend to us, but remains the police officer that he needs to be when he's investigating the mysteries and adventures that we get involved in."

Chapter 39

Running for the building, Muir looked back over her shoulder, tripping over her feet but managing to keep upright. She could hear the running footsteps behind her and reached for the door, yanking it open and flying through it and towards the security desk. Paul had looked up and then ran for the outside door, pointing towards the security office and ordering Muir inside and to lock the door.

Paul headed around the building, watching in frustration as the man ran away from him. He headed after him, Burnie following as he saw Paul.

"Paul?" Burnie finally caught up with him. "What's going on?"

"That man. He was chasing Muir. She made it into the building. I sent her to lock herself into the office." Paul was frustrated. "He got away. And I didn't get a good enough look at him to be able to describe him."

"No, I didn't either." Burnie spun and ran for the building, hammering at the office door, calling for Muir.

Muir stood, her back against the door, hearing Burnie calling for her, but too afraid to answer. She felt the door shoving against her as Paul opened it enough for Burnie to squeeze through. She flung herself into his arms, sobs breaking Burnie's heart as he listened to them. Paul headed for the desk, calling it in, but knowing that there wasn't much that the police would find.

Breck paced the conference room an hour later, the eyes of the men on him. The only one missing was Burnie and he had been adamant that he was not leaving Muir. Not just then. Barnabas had appeared, sent them off to their home, and then found Breck, calling a meeting with all the men.

Blair spoke up. "Breck, Barnabas? What happened?"

"Someone made an attempt to take Muir a while ago, from here on the property. She was able to get inside and Paul headed out. This is getting dangerous, fellows. We need to concentrate on solving this. I'm pulling you all back in to investigate." Barnabas had done this for each one of the men, knowing that their employers would be in agreement.

"Okay. What do we need to add to the whiteboards?" Brady was on his feet, heading that way, collecting papers on the way by the men.

"Has Emma been in touch?" Benen sorted through the papers that he had amassed.

"No, she's been quiet. I don't like that."

"She and Abe are away this week. They needed a break. Jace is working on everything, but he said he's got a lot on his plate." Bradon spoke up. "He's shooting me what he can later today. I'll get you all copies of it." He paused, a frown on his face. "That cousin of Holman's? Did we ever get any more information on him?"

"No, we didn't. It's like he didn't exist." Brendon looked up. "And somehow that's what I think we'll find. That he didn't really exist. Or else he's dead and someone is pretending to be him."

"Now, that would throw a curveball into it, wouldn't it?" Buckley looked up and then approached the boards. "Burnie was working this again like a logic problem, wasn't he?"

"We all were. He hasn't been doing a lot. He's had timelines that he has had to meet with his latest book." Brandon rose as well, heading to add information to another board. "I have found a link between Holman and Keafe."

"Keafe? How?"

"Holman approached Keafe a year ago and asked him to investigate something. Keafe refused. That is in the paperwork that Emma forwarded. I'm not sure how she found that."

"Likely from when she was investigating Ker's family." Brody looked up. "She does that. Finds connections, sets them aside, and then remembers them. I wish I had her memory."

"Me too. She's scary." Breck looked around as a tap came to the door and then a man looked in. "Can I help you?"

"You can. I'm looking for Burnie."

Breck walked towards him, Barnabas beside him. "He's not here. Can I ask your name?"

The man grinned as he pulled out his identification. "I'm Doug Foster. Cousin to Abe. He sent my wife and me to find Burnie and Muir."

"Doug? He's spoken of you." Breck reached to shake his hand. "Come on. I'll show you where he is."

Doug didn't move, his eyes on the walls. "I see that you have a nice setup."

"We do. We used to have paper, but then Barnabas had these installed." Breck looked over at Barnabas. "Barnabas?"

"Go on and find them, Breck. I'll stay here for now. Call if you need me."

Chapter 40

Burnie looked askance at the tall man and the lady with him that Breck had brought into his apartment. He knew Muir was in the office, he had left her there when he had answered the door.

"Burnie. This is Doug Foster and his wife, Darcie. Abe is cousin to Doug."

"Doug? Darcie? You have been mentioned. Glad to meet you." Burnie shot a look behind him. "I was about to make coffee but first, let me introduce you to Muir. We're in the office." Burnie led the way back, Muir rising to her feet, fear rising in her for a moment.

Burnie simply swung an arm around her. "Muir. This is Doug and Darcie. We talked about them."

"We did." Muir studied the couple before she focused on Darcie. "You did profiling."

Darcie grinned. "I did. I run a gift shop now." Her eyes went to the rainbow. "Oh, you have one of Ella's rainbows. She prays over each one she makes, that the new owner will be blessed by God."

"She does? That's why I feel such peace. Sit please." Muir sank back down onto the couch. "Tell me why you're here."

The three men walked away, conversation quiet between them. Doug was assessing Burnie and not liking the stress that he could see. He shared a look with Breck, who simply shook his head.

Muir watched Darcie for a moment. "Talk to me, please. I need help and I just can't seem to find the words to ask for it. Burnie is trying but I just don't want to burden him."

"Trust me, Muir. It is no burden for these fellows. You need to speak with him." Darcie reached for her hand, bowing her head to pray for Muir. When she looked up, she looked past Muir. "This man who held you?"

"Stewart? What about him?"

"He's older than you by about twenty years. He has been ruthless with so many people. Everyone is afraid of him. He resorts to violence and murder to get what he wants. His home life as a child was the same. Brutal. Full of violence. No love. Drugs and alcohol a large part of it. He saw an opportunity by chance when he saw a young woman abducted and taken overseas. He blackmailed the man who did it, making money to start doing it himself. Only he needed contacts and that he had to buy. You thwarted him, Muir. He will not forget that. He will come after you. To get to you, he will go after Burnie."

Muir drew in her breath. "I don't know how you did that, but that describes him. The man that held me? He was brutal and violent. I don't know how I survived, but for God. He told me exactly what he planned for me."

"I wondered." Darcie reached to hug her. "That's what they do. They beat down their victim, both physically and mentally, until there is no resistance. Part of their conditioning is to describe what will happen to them. I'm sorry, Muir, that it happened to you. You lost something through him that you should not have."

"I know. I get angry when I think of it, and have to pray for peace and for God to take vengeance. Is it wrong to ask that?"

"Not at all. He does say that vengeance is His. I saw that with what Doug and I went through. I almost died because of a bullet. Many people died because of the man who was responsible."

"You did? Oh, Darcie. How horrible!" Muir looked up as the men returned. "Burnie?"

"It's okay, sweetheart. Doug has some information from Abe and Emma that he needs to go over with us before we pass it on to Dallas and the fellows. But I know Breck. He wants to spend some time in prayer."

"That I do, Burnie. We need to cover you two with that. Doug? Will you lead us?"

Doug simply bowed his head and began to pray, Breck following and then Burnie, before Darcie took up the petition. When they were finished, there was a stillness in the room. Muir maintained afterwards that she could feel the presence of God in a powerful way, that He had spoken to her, to lead her to learn to trust Him deeper and fuller.

Chapter 41

Burnie headed into town the next morning, needing to mail documents to his publisher. He paused as he turned from the counter in the post office, not sure of the feeling of doom that suddenly overcame him. Lord, what is going on? I feel like I am at a crisis and don't know why or who.

He drove away, not seeing the car following him. There was enough traffic that the car could not get close enough to him to run him off the road, which had been their intent. The two men exchanged glances as they noted a patrol vehicle pull in front of them and then follow Burnie to the driveway of the Foundation property. The driver pounded at the steering wheel. They had missed a perfect opportunity, he complained loudly.

Burnie paused at the end of the driveway, watching as the car drove by and then returned, trying to catch the license plate number but unable to. He finally shook his head and drove forward, parking in his designated spot. He sat for a moment, puzzling over the car, before he shook his head. Another thought distracted him. Muir didn't drive. He wondered if she wanted to? He would have to ask her.

Brennen looked up as Burnie sat down beside him, his head tilting to watch his friend.

"Burnie?"

"I was followed. I think if the patrol vehicle had not moved in, I wouldn't be sitting here right now."

"That close?" Brennen whistled, catching Branigan's attention. "So, what do we do?"

"We keep a watch out, be as careful as we can be, and live life. Barnabas said that Morgan and McRae are heading back to Abe's for a time. He needs to debrief them as he calls it for the authorities overseas."

"How does Muir feel about that?" Branigan spoke up.

"I think she's relieved. She needs some time to absorb and accept what happened. Moira is quiet, too quiet. She's praying a lot, she said, but she's not talking a lot."

"None of them are. It was a brutal thing that happened. We're praying for them." Branigan's attention dropped to the paper that he had just picked up. "Burnie, when you were in the store, what did you see?"

"What do you mean?" Burnie sat back, his eyes on Branigan.

"Did you see anyone when you were in there? I mean, other than Muir and Holman?"

"No, not that I remember. Although I felt like someone else was there. Again, why?"

"Because in that pile of material that Emma sent? I found this." Branigan handed over a photo. "It's time stamped for around when you were in there."

Burnie took it, his eyes not leaving Branigan, who simply stared back at him. Burnie's eyes dropped to the photo, and he drew in a breath.

"There was someone else in there. I never saw him. He's standing near me. There was no one there. Just the three of us." Burnie looked up as he felt a hand on his shoulder.

Moira stood beside him, her eyes on the photo. "Michael? What is he doing there?"

"Michael?" Burnie shared a look with Branigan.

"Michael. He's the man who helped me to escape. Only he disappeared after he did. I never could find him."

"Moira, sit please." Burnie paused for a moment. "Have you and Muir discussed him?"

"We have. Muir decided that he was an angel. But I don't understand why he was there."

"To save Muir, I have no doubt. If we had been just a moment slower getting out of the store, we would have died. I felt a hand pushing me forward even as Muir and I ran. I shrugged it off as just stress and fear."

Moira shook her head, a slight smile on her face. "He gives us angels to protect us. I think Michael was provided just for Muir." She looked up. "Who to say that he wasn't there just for that reason, to get you out of the store in order for you two to survive?" She rose and walked away, leaving a stunned silence in the room.

The men gradually went back to what they had been working once, soberness in their hearts but wonder as well. Burnie rose and paced along the wall, reading what had been written. He sighed. This didn't seem to be getting him anywhere, he thought. Baird watched him before he too rose and came to walk beside him.

"What are your thoughts?"

"My thoughts? Who did Morgan anger that much? Was it because of Morgan or because of Muir? Would they really have watched her that long? I don't think so. Stewart didn't strike me as the sort of fellow who would. There has to be something that we're missing."

"I think the same. I just haven't been able to put a finger on it." Branigan reached for his phone as it chimed. "It's Emma. She sending you some more paperwork, Burnie. Although why she sent me the text and not you."

Burnie shrugged. "Does it matter if it moves us forward?" His voice died away and then he spun, reaching for a marker, moving to a clean board and frantically drawing and writing.

"Burnie?" Benen stood watching him.

"I'm plotting it out, Benen. Just like I might with a mystery story. That's how my mind thinks. Now, maybe I can make sense of it." He stepped back, his phone out to take a photo. "I need to talk to Muir and Moira but I'll do that later. Right now?" He reached for a different coloured marker and drew a line through the horizontal line he had already drawn. "If this was a story, this is where the crisis would occur. Right here. Right now. It would build to the climax.

Fellows, I think this is where it is going to get very dangerous. For all of us. Whoever it is may well go after anyone of us."

"I don't think so, Burnie." Brody spoke from where he stood beside Benen. "You're the one who stepped in, who stopped them. You're the one who walked away with Muir. Did we ever figure out why they had you handcuffed?"

"You know, I don't know that we did. Dallas didn't seem to be able to find out why." Burnie turned, a puzzled look on his face. "They tried to tell him it was because I was a material witness. You don't handcuff a material witness to a bed."

"No, you don't. They did that to keep you there. They thought that Muir would appear, to see how you were. If she had, then they would have nabbed her and had her disappear then." Breck spoke from where he stood just inside of the doorway. "There was always something off about that. I am glad that Muir had the sensibility to go to the airport and stow away. That got her out of there."

"It did." Burnie looked around, a thought niggling at his mind. "Breck? What was your sense of the airport there?"

"The airport? I'm not sure that I noticed much about it. It was small, not well maintained, but the planes were expensive." His words dropped off. "That's what you mean. The planes didn't fit the airport."

Burnie sighed. "I think that is exactly what I mean. I had noticed that when I drove into town and wondered about it. I think that there is more going on that what we have discovered. What if Muir was not to be sent overseas, but was being used to break her and then use her against her parents? Let them know that she was alive and that she would never be reunited with them unless they did something the men wanted?"

Chapter 42

Muir paced their living room later that day, her arms wrapped around herself. Burnie had been in, spoken briefly with her and then headed for his office downstairs. He had hated to do that but he had to write. He was driven to work on his manuscript, the words tumbling over one another in his mind. She returned to the kitchen, her finger lightly touching the photo that Emma had sent and that he had printed for her.

"There wasn't anyone else that I could see in the store. Just Stewart, Burnie and myself. But this is Michael, the man who helped Granny escape. Was I right? Was he an angel sent from God." Muir stopped speaking out loud, her eyes raising to the ceiling. "Was that You, God, looking after me?"

She then turned to the photo he had taken of the time line. She frowned. What was he after, Muir wondered? What was he looking for? She picked it up, returning to curl up on the couch, or sofa as Granny called it. Muir was puzzled. There was something missing, and she wasn't sure what.

Finally dropping the photo beside her, she reached for the Bible that Burnie had given her as a wedding gift. Muir's hand rubbed along the cover before she opened it, seeking verses that would calm her and then teach her to trust. That, she decided, was what she was needed. To learn to trust. And that came with difficulty.

Moira tapped at the door and then entered, watching Muir for a moment. She's been through so much, Lord, so much more than I would have ever expected. She needs this break from Morgan and McRae. I am not sure how they will ever become a family. There is too much time between them. Even I feel like I never knew them.

Muir looked up as her Granny sank down beside her, and then handed her the photo.

"Burnie did this. He plotted our adventure, as he calls it, out as a timeline in one of his novels. But there is something or someone missing. I just don't know who."

Moira studied it, before she tapped the photo. "He's really thought it out. But this here, where you ran for the airport? How much time passed by? I thought it was the next day."

Muir shook her head. "No. The explosion happened in the morning. I saw the plane landing that afternoon. Did Burnie ever say how they knew?"

"I'm not sure, child. That's something you'll need to ask him. But the plane? The airport was a ways from the store."

"I know. I had hidden in the trees and watched as they dragged Burnie away. Stewart kept calling for me. I just kept moving away from the store, away from town, and towards the airport. I don't know why I did that. I didn't want to go into town. I was that afraid. But I was worried about Burnie."

"I am sure that you were." Moira looked across the room, before she spoke. "Did you ever notice that the number of planes coming in had increased in the last years?"

"I did, Granny. They would come in, the men would go into town and then come back a few hours later. Why?"

"There had been rumours that there was an illegal gaming site there, for gambling." Moira watched her granddaughter. "Did any of the men ever come into the store?"

"Never. I couldn't understand that. I also couldn't understand why the store was off by itself like that."

"It hadn't been. Morgan had chosen a nice spot in town, but when he disappeared and Stewart took over, he moved it outside of town. There were protests that really didn't do much."

"I never knew that, Granny." Muir paled. "Was there something under the store?"

"What do you mean?"

"Like a tunnel or store room or something?" Muir searched frantically for her phone, finding it on the table beside her, and then sending off a text message to Dallas. "I'll ask Dallas. Maybe there was something there that he couldn't tell us."

"That's good." Moira's hand came out to stroke Muir's hair. "I'm sorry, Muir, that you had to undergo this. You shouldn't have had to."

"I know, Granny, but you always taught me that God was in control, that He allowed things and events."

"I know, child. That's what I believe. But to keep you from your parents for all these years? That's difficult to understand."

Muir shrugged, her eyes on the flowers on the coffee table in front of her. "I don't know that we will understand here on earth, Granny. But how do we do this? How do we stay safe and keep Burnie safe? Stewart is around. I can feel him. He'll go after Burnie for revenge."

"And you as well. We need to keep you safe, Muir." Moira was silent for a moment. "Did I ever tell you why you are called Muir?"

Muir stared at her for a moment before she shook her head. "I don't think so. I never thought about it, to tell you the truth."

"Muir was your mother's maiden name. In her family, it was tradition that the oldest girl took her mother's maiden name for her name. Your maternal grandmother was a McRae, that's how your mother got her name. And then your grandmother's name was McKenzie." Moira paused, a thought crossing her mind. "Have we traced back our trees, Muir? I don't remember doing that. Maybe there's something there."

"I thought of that, Granny. I emailed that Emma friend of Burnie. She got back to me right away. One of Abe's men? His wife has a family tree program. She had asked Emma for any information on us. I sent what I could. Emma said that she'd be back to me as soon as she could. Do you think there was something there?"

"Perhaps. It was always odd that your father and mother had to return to Ireland for business. As far as we knew, we had settled everything before we left."

"So they were enticed back there?" Muir shook her head. "I don't understand why." She looked up as she heard footsteps and Burnie and Blair appeared. "Burnie?"

"Muir. I think I have found a connection. Emma sent me some information. Kataleen, a friend, is working on your background, she said, but she wanted me to have this." Burnie held out a sheet of paper. "Your family is connected years ago with Holman."

"We are?" Muir paled. "We're related? Is that why?"

Chapter 43

Burnie paced the conference room later that day, his friends watching him. He was puzzled. How had Kataleen traced that back, he wondered? He wasn't sure how she did what she did, but he was unsettled. Muir and Moira had not said much and that concerned him.

"Burnie?" Branigan waited for Burnie to turn towards him before he held out the sheaf of papers that he was holding. "You need to see these."

"And these are?" Burnie took them, his eyes on Branigan.

"Confirmation that there was a cellar to the store. Muir asked Dallas about it. He just got back to me. He tried to reach you."

Burnie sighed. "I muted my phone when I was writing. I need to stop doing that."

"Yes, you do. It could mean your life or Muir's." Branigan simply shook his head and walked away.

Burnie returned to the chair he favoured, dropping the papers to the desk, and praying first. He read through them, looked at the photos, and then raised his head. "What was the meaning of this room?" He was puzzled. The room, Dallas noted, was empty and had been cleaned recently. The techs had not picked up on anything there, or had the dogs that had been brought in.

"Puzzled, Burnie?" Blair sat beside him.

"I am. Muir questioned if there was a room or something under the store. Dallas has confirmed that there was and provided photos that he said could be released to us. I didn't think that he could."

"If they're not relevant, then he likely cleared it. May I?" Blair reached for the photos. "These are interesting." He frowned. "There were shelves there. You can see the spots on the walls."

"I noticed that. I wonder what they had down there."

"Something illegal for sure." Blair leaned closer to the photo and then paled. "Burnie? Did you see this?"

"See what?" Burnie had already moved on to new research.

"Here? The shackles?"

"What?" Burnie stared at Blair before he reached for the photos. He paled. "Shackles. Who did they have down there?"

"Somehow, I think they would have put you down there, if the fellows hadn't turned up. Who called Barnabas?"

"You know, I'm not sure that I was told." Burnie frowned. "And we can't ask him. He's away for a couple of days, he said."

"He is. Breck might know." Blair was on his feet, heading out of the room, to try and track down Breck. He was back in short order, returning to sit beside Burnie. "It was an anonymous call, just that you were in trouble and someone needed to come rescue you."

"Michael?"

"Michael? It might have been, but it could have been anyone in the town." Blair frowned. "I guess it's not relevant."

"But it could be." Burnie pointed to the timeline that he had created. "I added some stuff. I'm not sure how far or deep to probe."

"As far as we need to. Burnie? Has Muir talked much more about what it was like? Don't tell me if it's confidential."

Burnie shrugged. "She's not saying much. She's burying it and I don't like that. I have tried to get her to talk, but she's not ready to. Not yet." He buried his face into his hands. "This is so hard."

"We know, Burnie. We know. We are praying for both of you. Has Buckley talked with you?"

Burnie nodded, as he looked up, a bleak look around his eyes. "He has. And Locklin has been talking with Muir. And I know that Darcie has been calling Muir every day. Muir says that helps, that Darcie is able to give her advice and a perspective that no one else can." Burnie sat back, his eyes on Blair. "How do I help her?"

"By doing what you're doing. Loving her. Letting her have her space. Let her rage and cry and scream if she needs to."

"You went through that with Devaney?"

"I did. Even now, there are times when it all comes back. With our little one almost here, she's finding her emotions are all over the place."

"I can understand that." Burnie stopped for a moment. "Blair, if it was you, what would you do? What would you look into?"

"Me? I would start with Morgan and McRae. It just seems odd that they didn't make any attempt to escape, not until now. Who did they talk to over there? And if they talked, why didn't it go any further?"

Burnie pointed a finger at Blair. "There. That's what has me puzzled. Why now? Why not before? Emma might have an idea. I'll call her." He was on his feet, almost running from the room, heading for his office, needing the silence that he would find there and the privacy that he needed.

Chapter 44

Burnie finally set his phone now, determination on his face. He had just had a long conversation with Emma and Kataleen who had been there. The two ladies had thought of questions that he hadn't known he needed to ask. He stared at the myriad pages of notes that he now had to make sense of. He glanced at the clock and rose, gathering his papers and heading for his home.

Muir turned as he entered, coming towards him eagerly for his hug and kiss, and then just standing, their arms wrapped around one another, feeling the doom that was gathering over them.

"Burnie? You have changed. What happened?" Muir leaned back to look up at him.

"We'll talk, sweetheart. But you have lunch ready for us?"

"I do. Breck was by. He was looking for you." She turned to ladle out the soup that she had heated.

"He was? I'll catch up with him later."

The meal over, Burnie rose to clear the table, his hand on Muir's shoulder keeping her in her chair. Then he sat once more, his hands reaching for hers, his head bowing as he prayed for them, a desperation in his prayer that Muir had not heard before.

"Burnie?" Muir raised her head, to find him staring at the papers in front on him.

193

"Muir? You said that your family had been tracked back to Holman. It's not the Holmans here that you are related to. They are a totally separate branch. Stewart had tried to take advantage of your lack of knowledge. I had a long conversation with Emma and Kataleen just a while ago. This is what came from it." He tapped the papers. "We need to sort through it all before I talk to the fellows. I think this will help a lot."

"So, where do we start?" Muir reached for the papers, sorting through them, and then beginning reading. "I didn't know that Dad was one of the founders of the village. Granny never said."

"We'll ask her, but I don't think that it was common knowledge. He had been approached by a friend to move here and do that. They had drawn up a village charter, set the details out for a village constabulary as he called it. I don't know where Emma found all this, but she did. She'll forward it to us and to Dallas. It helps to explain Stewart's motivation."

"It does. He wanted to be rich. He would tell me that. It angers me that he did what he did to me. And to Mom and Dad." Muir sat back, a thought passing through her mind. "How do we know for sure that they are Mom and Dad?"

"Emma said Abe thought of that and has asked for DNA samples from them. They have been resisting."

"And that makes them suspects, doesn't it? Are they even my parents or are they imposters?"

"At the moment, they are suspects and that's why Abe pulled them back to where he could watch them.

194

He doesn't trust them. He'll keep them on his Rebel's compound for now. He's working with both the force here, the force in his town, and the authorities overseas. It's a priority for him. Emma said he'd be sending someone over to talk with us at some point over the next few days."

"I'm getting tired of talking. I want this over with. How do we do just that? Put ourselves out as targets?"

Burnie grinned at the disgruntled look on her face. "We could do that, but I think Dallas would want to be involved in the planning. For now, we stick close to here."

"And it's not much safer, is it?" Muir rose, heading for the kettle to make herself another cup of tea, reaching to refill Burnie's mug of coffee, before she reached for the plate of cookies sitting on the counter. "I worry about Granny."

"I know. I do too. Emma talked to me. They would like to have her come and visit them, staying with some friends who don't live on their property."

"They would do that?" Muir finally nodded. "We should get her to do that. But it might be difficult."

"Emma has approached her already. She is agreeable."

"Emma did? What doesn't Emma do?"

"Emma and Abe had their own adventure as did all of his men and many friends of theirs. I trust him to keep her safe."

"When?" Muir's voice was barely above a whisper, knowing that she would be going through the next while without the stability that her Granny had provided.

"Soon, Muir. Soon." Burnie simply reached to draw her to himself. "I'll do my best to step up and keep you safe. So will all the fellows. It's what we do for one another."

Muir nodded against him. "I know, Burnie, but it's hard. The six months that she was out of my life were so long. Not just because of what I went through."

"We now, sweetheart. We know. We'll do our best. Right now, let's pray. I need to learn to trust even more than I do."

"I need to see Granny." Muir began to sob, her heartbreaking weeping breaking Burnie's heart as he held her, finally shoving back his chair enough to simply draw her to his knee and weep with her. Muir's tears finally stopped, but she made no effort to move from him.

"Muir? I love you more each day. I will do my utmost to keep you safe." Burnie bit at his lip. "Right now, it's what we know to be the most dangerous part of this. Stewart will be after both of us. We don't know who else is involved, so we have to be extra cautious. We still live. We go about our normal daily walk. We go out for dinners, on dates. We work."

"I understand, Burnie." Muir's voice was still tear-filled. "But it's dangerous for anyone around us."

"We know that, too, Muir. We take as many precautions as we can." Burnie's head tilted as he watched her. "Right now, I'm happy just to hold you and comfort you. But we do need to work."

"I know." Muir sighed. "What can I do to help you? Am I banned from the conference room?"

"Absolutely not. Here. Let's wash your face and we'll head down there. In fact, I think it's a great idea that you're down there. We sometimes have questions that we need to set aside. If you're there, we can ask right away."

Chapter 45

Two days later, Muir walked along the wall in the conference room, studying the material and noting the new information that had been added. She stopped at the logic problem, her finger up to trace the questions and names. She frowned. What had they been trying to discover, she wondered? Brody stood near her.

"Muir? You're puzzled by the puzzle?" He grinned as she frowned at him.

"I am. I don't understand what you were trying to discover. It doesn't make sense."

Brody nodded. "Sometimes things don't." He reached to hand her a marker and pointed to a clean board. "How be you try one?"

"Me? Make up a puzzle? I'm puzzle enough without that. Besides, I wouldn't now what to ask."

"Just write down what is puzzling you. Then work from that." Brody turned to walk away, stopping as Muir asked him to stay.

"I need your help, Brody. I don't understand how this all works, but I'll give it a try." Muir stepped back after a while, the board covered in her neat handwriting. "I did all that?"

"You did, Muir. You did. You think out loud, do you know that?" Brody grinned as he held up a pad of paper. "I made notes."

"You did? Care to share?"

"Certainly.   There are some things here that aren't on the board." Brody looked up as Buckley and Benen approached. "Muir's working on her own logic problem. She didn't like ours."

"Yours is okay. It just didn't make sense to me." Muir read through Brody's notes, pausing at one comment. "I said that? Stewart had no sister, not that I know of. Why would I refer to her?"

"A lady?" Benen reached for the notes. "When was this?"

"I think about eight months ago. She was around for about a week. He introduced her as his sister, even though we all knew that he only had a brother." Muir paled. "What happened to her?"

"Did you have a name?"

Muir shook her head. "No, no name. He just called her his sister. Funny thing is that he wouldn't let her out of his sight."

"No, I don't think he would. Can you describe her?"

Muir did that, not catching the glances that the men were exchanging.

Burnie stopped beside her, an arm around her. "Muir, this lady? Do you know how much she resembles you?"

Muir turned her head to watch him. "No, not really. She was only five foot tall, if that. And heavier.

Her hair was the wrong colour. I think it had been dyed. And her eyes were strange."

"Contact lenses, then." Brody made notes. "I wonder if she was there as a captive or as someone who was in control. It may have looked as if Holman was keeping her in his control. What if it was the other way around? She was watching him, keeping him in her control?"

"I would hazard a guess that's what it was." Brendon reached for the papers, reading through them. "I want a copy of this. Do you mind, Brody?"

"No, go ahead. Make a copy for Dallas as well."

Muir walked back along the wall, the marker in her hand underlying certain events and statements. Brandon watched her, before he turned to Burnie.

"Burnie? What's she doing?"

"Making sense of it all. I think that we were remiss in trying to protect her from being here. She's driven so much down inside that I think it will all come out at once." Burnie watched her closely once more. "I wonder what she's found."

Muir turned back to Burnie, walking into his arms and hugging him. "I found out who it is, Burnie. It's been there all along. I just needed to follow the steps."

"You know who it is?" Burnie looked up at the sudden silence in the room.

"I do. Everything that I have underlined? Write it all down in the order that I numbered it. Then we talk. Right now, I need to see Granny and she's already left."

"I'm sorry, Muir. She has. What can we do?"

"Just find this monster. He's here somewhere, I just know." Muir sank into a chair, her head going down on her folded arms, her body shuddering from the deep sigh that she drew.

Chapter 46

Her hand tight in Burnie's, Muir wandered along the sand by Lake Erie, her hair tossed by the light wind that had come up. She was amazed at the sight of the lake, watching the waves roll in.

Burnie grinned at her smile, knowing that this was what she had needed, to do something that took her away from her thoughts. He reached to kiss her, and then pointed to a lake freighter.

Muir nodded, her eyes on Burnie instead. Lord, I am afraid. I am afraid for my man, that something is going happen and happen today. How do we stop that? Or do we? Do we really have to go through more danger and trials and troubles? I know that You are here with us and if You chose, nothing would happen. But sometimes we need those trials in order to grow. Teach me to trust You as I should.

Burnie hesitated for a moment and then turned their steps back towards the pathway to the building.

"Having fun, sweetheart?"

"I am." Muir nodded. "I needed this. There is something calming about watching the waves. I want to see this lake in the middle of a storm, to remember that I know Who it is who calms them."

"We can do that. Late fall is a good time for that. We can get gale-force winds at that time."

"Burnie? Have you heard from Granny?"

"No, I haven't. Abe said that would likely be the case. To try and hide her away somewhere that she couldn't be used against you." Burnie sighed, knowing what she was asking. "If something had happened to her, he would have been in touch."

"I know. I just need to speak with her." Muir's eyes raised to the trees that they were asking under. "How many paths are there to the lake?"

"A few. Some go through the fields and clearings around us. This is my favourite one. But somehow, I think I made a mistake." He suddenly began to run, heading for home, Muir's flying feet keeping step with him.

Burnie slid to a halt as a man appeared in their path, a weapon held on them. He tried to back up, feeling a weapon against his back. His free hand raised, his other hand keeping a tight grip on Muir.

"What do you want?"

"You two. You're coming with us." The man motioned with his weapon. "Now, head off that way. And no funny stuff."

Muir's hand tightened on Burnie as they moved away, away from the safety of the building and their friends, away towards what, they didn't know. They were forced to walk for a couple of miles before they were shoved into a cave and then deeper into another cave. Burnie's arm came around Muir, as they stood, staring at the empty entrance, but knowing that the men were still out there. They could hear their movements.

"Muir? If you get a chance, run. Head back the way we came. I know this area. If you head towards the tallest pine tree that you can see, that's where our building is."

"Not without you." Muir's imploring look almost broke his heart.

"I need you to do that for me. Promise? I'll be right behind you. That I will try to do."

Burnie paced the cave, his eyes on the entrance before flickering to Muir, watching as she huddled on the floor, her arms wrapped around herself. He sighed. That was not a good idea, he thought, going to the lake. How did he get word to the others? He had let Baird know what they were doing and giving him a time that they should return. Baird would check on them and then head for help to come and find them. Please, Lord, let my lady live and get away.

Burnie listened closely late that afternoon, hearing nothing from the other cave. He walked that way, Muir's hand on his back. He stopped, listening, and then peered outside. He couldn't see the men.

"Run, Muir. Head for home. I'm right behind you." Burnie shoved at her, watching as she ran, before he ran after her.

A sudden sharp pain in his chest drove him backwards and to the ground, where he lay, sprawled on his back, an arrow protruding from his chest. The world disappeared into a swirling darkness as he lost consciousness. He didn't hear Muir's scream or feel her hands on him, trying to rouse him. Burnie didn't see the men who stood over them before one of them pulled Muir to her feet and away from him. She began to fight him, breaking free and running, the sound of his pounding feet coming after her.

Muir searched for some place to hide, not finding anything, her fear spurring her on. She gave a scream as the land dropped off in front of her before she plunged over a cliff, to lie in a sprawled, motionless heap on a pile of evergreens. The man following her peered over and then nodded, moving away, a smile of satisfaction on his face. There was no way that she'd survive that, he decided. He ran back the way that he had come, finding his companion ready to leave.

"He's not going to be going anywhere." The man's voice was gruff. "Let's get out of here? What about her?"

"Ran over a cliff. She's likely dead. I'm not going down to find out. Let's move." They disappeared, leaving the two forms crumpled and appearing lifeless behind them.

Chapter 47

Pounding at Burnie's door, Brody finally just rested his hand against it. There was no answer, just as there had been no answer at Burnie's office door. It was past time that Burnie thought that they would be back. Burnie, where are you? Brody turned and ran for the conference room, the door flying open as he ran in.

"Brody?" Barnabas was on his feet.

"Burnie and Muir. They went for a walk towards the lake. I tried to talk him out of it. They were to be home by now and aren't. I can't get an answer at his office or his apartment."

The men were on their feet, flying from the room, heading to dress for the weather and their search, backpacks in place as they met in the parking lot.

"We'll pray and then split up into teams, each team taking a path." Barnabas led them off in prayer and then watched as they scattered. "Bradon? You're ready with Kade?"

"I am. We're taking the path through the woods?"

"We are. He likes that one, I know."

Kade suddenly alerted, drawing Bradon's attention before he tugged at his leash, wanting to head away from the lake.

"He's hit on something, Barnabas. I say let's follow him."

"I agree. I don't like this, Bradon. Rain is moving in."

"It is. Let's move ourselves."

Kade surged ahead, suddenly stopping before he gave a loud bark and then frantically tried to move away from Bradon. Bradon dropped the leash, watching as Kade ran forward, not waiting for his master to follow.

"He's hit on something." Barnabas ran after him, following Bradon.

"It's Burnie." Bradon was on his knees, shoving Kade away. "An arrow?"

"An arrow. Who did that?" Barnabas looked around. "No sign of Muir. Where is she?"

"I don't know, but I'm calling in." Bradon did that, and then shoved his pack from his back, pulling out a folded emergency blanket and wrapping it around Burnie. "He's not coming to at all, Barnabas."

"I know." Barnabas knelt beside his friend, his hand resting on his arm, even as a prayer wafted heavenward for him.

Thirty minutes later, the two men stood back, watching as the emergency personnel worked on Burnie, and the officers searched the area.

"Burnie would not have left her, not on his own." Brady spoke up. "Where is she? Bradon, can Kade track her?"

"Likely." Bradon moved away from the commotion, then hand on Kade's head, gave the command to find Muir. "Go, boy. Find Muir."

Kade raised his head, gave a woof, and then started his search, heading towards the cliff, intent on following the scent that he associated with Muir.

"Oh, no! The cliff!" Breck ran towards it, followed by most of the men, sliding to a halt as he watched Kade alert at the edge. He gripped a hand and leaned over. "I see her. She's not moving."

"Can I get down there?" Brady was on his knees, looking over. "It's not that far. Six or seven feet." He was over the edge, dropping and rolling as he landed, before he scrambled towards Muir, a hand reaching for a pulse. "She's alive, fellows. But I'll need a backboard and neck collar."

"On it!" Breck ran back towards where the emergency personnel were still working on Burnie, ready to move him. "We found Muir! She's over the cliff. Brady needs a backboard and collar!"

The men spun, one running towards him, one running for the rig parked not far away, even as the other two paramedics lifted Burnie's stretcher and moved away as rapidly as they could.

Two hours later, Barnabas paced the waiting room in the Emergency room. The men from the building paced as well, both inside and outside. The ladies had gathered in the chapel, praying for their friends, Anna with them. Doc was on duty in the department, appearing briefly just to let them know that Burnie and Muir were being taken care of.

Dallas appeared and then headed back to speak with Doc, not liking the report that Doc gave him. It was grave enough for Burnie, but with Muir, they were still awaiting imaging studies to be reported, he said. He had simply shaken his head at Dallas and then pointed him away. Emergency was busy that day, and Doc was rushed. They didn't see the men standing in the corner of the waiting room, eyeing the doorway to the examination rooms. Breck finally pulled Barnabas aside.

"What is Doc not saying?" Breck kept his eyes on the waiting room, watching carefully.

"I don't know. You know Doc. He's careful with patient confidentiality. I suspect that until he has permission from Moira to talk about Muir, he won't. Do you know if she's her next of kin?"

"I have a call into Abe. He's faxing something in once he's talked to her, to let them speak with you or I."

"Good. I hate this, Breck. All of the men have ended up here at some point."

"I know. That just leaves you and me, you know."

"I know." Barnabas grew silent, his mind drifting back in time before he shook his head. "I always feel like there has been something left hanging, though."

"I know what you mean. I think that there is." Breck nodded towards Doc as he headed for them. "Here's Doc. I'll just step away."

"Breck, stay. You're named in the document that Moira signed." Doc sighed, getting tired of treating his young friends. "She's given permission for me to talk to you both. Until Burnie is able to make decisions, she has asked that you or Breck do, Barnabas. Abe will bring her here if we need her to be."

"And do we?" Barnabas prayed that was not the case.

"Not yet. And I don't know that we will. What did Muir land on?"

"A pile of evergreen branches." Breck shared a look with Barnabas. "But how did they get there? There shouldn't have been."

"God again." Doc pointed to the outside. "Let's walk for a moment. I need a breath of fresh air." He tucked his reading glasses into his pocket.

After a few minutes, Doc began to talk, to detail Burnie's injuries.

"The arrow missed anything vital, even to blood vessels. He's being stitched up by the surgeon in the exam room. He's been awake and refused to leave there, wanting to get up and find Muir."

"Of course, he would. Muir?" Barnabas was almost afraid to ask.

"Now, Muir. I have no explanation, Barnabas, Breck. She's battered and bruised. She knocked herself out somehow, but she has not internal injuries. No broken bones. I can't explain it."

"That's God at work, Doc." Breck blinked rapidly. Muir had become like a sister to him, as had all the ladies. "Thank God. But I can't explain how the branches ended up there."

"Nor can I. They shouldn't have been." Barnabas stared at the pavement in front of his feet. "Someone prepared that, knowing that Muir would run that way. I'm not going to probe it any further."

"No, I don't think we can. Give us some time and I'll get you both in to see them. They can go home today."

Chapter 48

Burnie moved carefully through the apartment the next day, his arm in sling to prevent the muscles from pulling. He sighed. This is not what he needed, not at this time. He turned as he heard Muir moving around in the bedroom and headed that way, finding her sitting on the side of the bed. He sat beside her, an arm around her.

"Muir?"

She nodded, sniffing, wiping at the tears on her face before she leaned against him.

"I'm tired of this, Burnie. I'm tired of being chased and hurt and destroyed. For what? We haven't even figured that out. I talked to Dallas a few moments ago, when you were in the shower. He's heading this way. He wants to talk to us. All we seem to do is talk."

Burnie dropped a kiss on her head. "I know, sweetheart. It's hard. It's hard to trust at times like this."

"It is. I keep praying this to be over." She wiped her hands along her jeans. "I heard from Kataleen. She said she's sending more material to us."

"She is? Did she say anything?"

Muir nodded. "She's proven that Stewart is not in our line at all. So what he was saying was all talk. She also said she was sending a document that we needed to look at together. She refused to say what it was, only that she was praying for us."

"She did, did she? That's what getting us through, you know. The prayers of our church and the prayers of our friends." Burnie grew quiet, not sure what to say.

"Burnie, what would have happened if you had not been there? Given what we know now, was I to be sent overseas?"

"I doubt it. I think it was all talk on Stewart's part. He wanted to control you, and keep you down and in the store. He didn't pay you, did he?"

Muir shook her head. "No, he said he provided room and board. That was all I could expect to get." She grew angry for a moment. "I let him do that to me."

"You didn't have an escape."

"Not until you and your friends showed up. Did Dallas ever say anything more about what they found?"

"No, he hasn't. I asked him. He said it was still in the preliminary investigation stage. That there was a lot of work to do. Ker wonders if some of the teens that disappeared from her town ended up there."

"That's sad, you know. I guess that's the evil that we have around us. God protects us, I know that, but there is just so much evil." Muir finally rose, heading for the kitchen, reaching for her tea that Burnie had made for her. She turned as she heard his footsteps. "How's your shoulder?"

"It hurts and will for a while. The surgeon said I was lucky. I told him it was God. He just stared at me."

"We've been able to witness to others through all this, haven't we? Even the others have commented that they have been able to share with the medical staff and others." Muir sipped at her cooling tea. "Burnie, when this is all over, do we stay here?"

"Here? As in the building?" At her nod, he simply hugged her. "If you want. I would like to. It's been my home for many years. But if you feel you want to move, I will do that."

"You would?" Muir tilted her head back to look up at him. "No, I love the building here. The family that we have. I never had that, other than Granny."

"Then we stay." The young couple stood for a while. "I would like to take you away for a vacation, belated honeymoon, whatever you want to call it, when this is over."

"You would? Where?"

He shrugged. "I have no idea. Ireland?"

Muir shook her head. "No, I don't think so. This is my country. I have always wanted to go to the Maritimes."

"Then, we'll head there. There are lots of areas that we can explore. And we can take day trips here in Ontario. And when I get to travel for my books, you come with me."

"I do?"

"You do." Burnie stepped back, a frown on his face as he heard a tap at the door. "We're we expecting anyone?"

Muir shrugged. "Not that I know of, but it's become like a train or bus station lately."

Burnie was laughing at her comment as he opened the door, to find Barnabas and Breck standing there, Branigan with them, and Abe coming along the hallway.

"Fellows? Come on it. The coffee's on, but somehow I don't think that you're here for coffee."

"We can be, but we need to speak with both of you. Dallas is about five minutes out, he said." Breck hugged Muir on the way by. "And how are you, Muir?"

"Sore and puzzled."

"You are? About what?"

"About that pile of evergreens. Who put them there?"

"God. That's the only explanation that we can come up with." Branigan gave her a hug as well, before reaching for the mug that Breck was extending to him. "Can we meet in the office or the living room?"

"Office, I think, Branigan. That way, if we need the computer, we'll have it." Burnie reached for Muir's hand, finding hers cold.

Chapter 49

Muir sat beside Burnie, her hand tight in his, watching the other men carefully. Breck had taken a seat at Burnie's computer, after Burnie had signed in, ready to search if needed. Abe had simply shaken his head and handed over the folder that he had brought with him.

Burnie had taken it, a frown on his face, then bowed his head as Abe prayed. The other men followed, Branigan bringing it to a close. They sat for a few moments before Burnie opened the folder, staring down at the picture.

"These are the people who said that they were Muir's parents."

"They are. They look enough like them to fool even Moira. Although Moira has said that something seemed off about them. She put that down to being so many years."

"But it's not, is it?" Muir leaned against Burnie and frowned. "I see what you mean, Burnie. They aren't my parents." She was on her feet, running from the room and then returning with a faded photograph. "These are my parents. Who are these people?"

"Actors that were hired. They had to undergo plastic surgery to alter their looks. They were paid well enough that they agreed to it." Abe looked at Muir. "I'm sorry, Muir, for our part in this."

"You didn't know? How could you?" Muir watched him. "But you had hesitation, didn't you? That's why you removed them."

"You're correct, Muir. Something just seemed off to all of my men. We agreed that we needed to pull them away. We have been in constant contact with the Irish authorities. The couple finally confessed last night as to what they had been hired to do." Abe looked dpwm before he looked up at Muir, sorrow in his eyes. "I'm sorry, Muir. We have confirmation that there was a plane crash on a remote island. Your parents' remains have been discovered. If you wish, we can return them here for you to bury."

"Talk to Granny. I'll abide by what she said. Who?" Muir's voice had dropped to a whisper. She didn't remember her parents, so to bury them here was not really a thought that she had had.

"We have. She has said to bury them in the family plot in Ireland."

Muir nodded, before she reached to flip the photo over. "Who is this person?"

"That's what we're finding out. He was a business partner of your father. In fact, he is the one who your father was to meet with when he returned to Ireland. This man? He's skirted close to the edge of the law all his life. We are surmising that is why your father moved away. He was trying to draw your father into illegal activities and was making it difficult for your father to continue to live in your home town."

"I see. You know, he looks like Stewart. Are they related?"

"You have a good eye, Muir." Burnie turned to the next page. "He's a nephew of the man. How did he end up here?"

"He was sent over before your father came over. Holman sent him over. And yes, the man's name is Holman. We talked to Moira. She had never know the man's name, only knew of him. Your father had never given the name." Abe looked up as Dallas appeared, Branigan having gone to the door.

"Dallas?" Muir looked up at him, seeing the fatigue in his face. "You're here."

Dallas grinned for a moment. "I am. I need to talk to you as well."

They talked for a while longer before everyone but Dallas left. He sat back, his eyes closing for a moment.

"Dallas? You needed to talk to us?" Burnie spoke quietly

Dallas nodded before his eyes opened. "I do. Muir, I regret to inform you that Stewart Holman was killed in a hit and run last night. We just got word this morning."

"He's dead?" Muir was shocked. "Now what?"

"Now we continue to piece together the parts that aren't. We're still a long ways away from that. I can't stress how much you two need to still practice safety."

"We know that, Dallas. What else?" Muir watched him closely.

"One of his known associates is in town. He's asking about you and Burnie." Dallas sighed. "The people on the street aren't talking. They respect the Foundation too much to do that, the Foundation having helped out many of them over the years. He knows where the building is. He was followed here one day. We had no reason to stop him."

"I see. So that leave us vulnerable?" Burnie shut his eyes, picturing a possible scenario. "How do we go on the offensive, Dallas? I want this over."

"We've been discussing that with our PR people. We could do a television interview, but they think just a statement issued by them will help. It means that it will draw out whoever it is and they will come after you even harder."

"We understand, Dallas, but we can't continue to live as we are. It's not fair to Muir."

Dallas finally rose, his eyes on the couple before he walked away. They're planning something, aren't they, Lord? Protect them.

Chapter 50

The next morning, Muir paced the walkways in the garden, Burnie keeping step with her. They had spent the night in prayer and made a decision to go on the offensive. They had stopped in the conference room before they came out, the men listening to their plans, discussing it, adding to it. She knew that some of the men were hidden around them, as were some of the security team. That they were taking a risk, she knew. She just prayed that no one was hurt.

"Burnie, are we doing the right thing?" Muir looked up at him.

He nodded. "I think so. I pray so. We had peace about it, Muir, when we left the conference room. I pray that it ends today. I know that there will be investigations to complete, court to face, but if we can trap the men and the ones responsible then it's over."

Muir sighed. "I just wish it was all over. I hate living like this. Stewart has taken so much from me. His uncle took much more. Did they arrest him?"

"They have. They found all sorts of information that the authorities over there will be working through. They also found confirmation that you were a target, just because. Apparently in the town bylaws, you would take over the biggest portion of the town when you turn thirty. They were trying to prevent that. They had a nice little scheme going."

"I was? Does Granny know that?"

"Abe was going to speak with her, but Dallas asked him not to. He wants Moira to return here and then he's planning on talking with both of you."

"I see." Muir's footsteps slowed. "Burnie?"

"Yes, love." When Muir didn't respond, he looked up, a frown on his face before it cleared. "Of course, Dennis Holman. I never connected you."

The man, in his late sixties, stood in front of them, a heavy walking stick in his hand. His face was a true picture of pure evil as he glared at them.

"You should have. That oversight will cost you dearly." He motioned to Muir. "Walk towards me. Now!" His voice rose as she retreated. "I said, walk towards me."

Muir simply shook her head and retreated some more, Burnie moving with her. "I don't think so. I remember seeing you in the store and around the village. I didn't know who you were, though."

"No, we kept that carefully from you and your granny. It wouldn't have made any difference. You see, you've just written a will, deeding your property there to me when you die. Not to your husband or anyone else. It belongs to me. It should have all along." The man's face grew more cruel as he paced carefully towards her, his limp pronounced as he held his walking stick up high.

"I don't think so. I wouldn't do that." Muir screamed as the heavy stick landed on her shoulder, sending her to the ground in horrible pain. She heard Burnie cry out and then there was silence.

Burnie was on his knees beside her before he swept her up and ran for the infirmary, Brady beside him. Brady's hands were gentle as he felt her shoulder.

"Broken?" Burnie was afraid, his own chest hurting from the movement and weight of carrying his sweetheart to safety.

"I don't think so. She was moving down when he struck at her. Kade took him down before he really hit her hard."

"Thanks to Kade, once more. We own him a nice raw steak dinner." Burnie's hand rested on Muir's face. "Do we need X-Rays?"

Brady nodded. "We will. Let me talk to the officers who are out there. One of them will take us in." He was back in short order. "Okay, let's move, Burnie. We have an escort. I'm driving and you're with me."

Muir turned restlessly that night, her shoulder paining her, before she stilled, watching Burnie as he slept, her head pillowed on his shoulder before she too slept. Dallas had called just as they were heading off for the night, weariness in his voice, but jubilance as well. He had stated that Holman was the head of it all, and that they would be arresting everyone else over the next day or so. Could the two of them just stay out of trouble for a bit, he pleaded.

Chapter 51

A week later, Burnie sat in the conference room, his sling gone, his arm around his sweetheart, pulling her tight to him. She smiled up at him, peace on her face at long last. It had been a long time coming, he thought. Dallas had asked for the meeting. Now, to find out why and who.

Dallas entered finally, Will Peters with him, a sheaf of folders in his hands that he dropped onto a nearby table. He searched the room, finding Moira and heading towards her.

"Moira? I am sorry about Morgan and McRae."

Moira nodded before she reached to hug him. "I knew it wasn't them, but I couldn't be sure. It had been too long. I am glad that we know where they are now. It will give us closure." She looked towards Muir. "Muir is happy, and that makes me happy. I have not told Muir yet, but I'm moving into an apartment in town. I need to. For my sake and for hers. She has a life now with Burnie."

"They won't want you to." Dallas reached to hug her again. "They will want you nearby."

"I know that, but they need this time to themselves. They're newlyweds. They need to learn about one another without an old woman interfering."

"Not interfering, Moira. You have become Granny to all of us here. All of the men but Breck and

223

Barnabas have no family. Some of the ladies as well. The little ones who are coming will be delighted to have a great-granny to spoil them."

"I know that, Dallas, but I can do that from town. It's time for me to move on." Moira nodded towards the front. "I think that they are waiting for you."

Dallas moved to the front, pausing beside Buckley. "Buckley, will you? I know that it's Barnabas' place to ask you."

"He already has. Thank you, Dallas, for what you've done for all of us. I know it's been a strain on you. I can tell you're wearing out."

"I am, Buckley. I am trying to make a decision and would appreciate your prayers."

"You have had them." Buckley was on his feet, moving to the front, waiting for the room to quiet before he prayed, a powerful prayer that seemed to lift them right up to the throne of God. He waited for a moment when he finished before he raised his head, his eyes on Muir, frowning. No, he was seeing things. There was not someone standing behind her. He blinked, and the person had disappeared.

Barnabas rose, his eyes roaming the room. The men and ladies of the building have been through so much, Lord, some almost dying. You have protected them, strengthened them, and brought them their life partners. His eyes turned to Breck, who stood at the back of the room, leaning against the wall. For my old friend, Breck, Lord, I sense that he is next and that he too will face danger. Protect him, Lord. And for myself? You know what I wish. Grant it if it be Your will.

Barnabas finally cleared his throat and spoke, talking with each couple before he came to Burnie and Muir.

"Burnie. Muir. What can I say? God has provided for and protected you. Muir, you are a welcome part of our family, Burnie's helpmeet. He has waited his whole life for you. Now, it's my turn to be quiet and let Dallas speak. Before I do, I just want to thank each one of you fellows and the ladies for your dedication to helping solve each mystery or adventure. For the support that you have shown. For the prayers that have been raised." Barnabas grew quiet, his hand motioning to Dallas, before he walked to the back of the room, to stand shoulder to shoulder with Breck. Breck's hand rested on his shoulder for a moment before they turned to listen to Dallas.

Barnabas' eyes were on Muir and Burnie, watching them closely. Lord, is this over for them, or is there something else? He drew in a breath and abruptly left the room, running for his office, pulling up an email from Emma that he printed. He ran once more for the conference room, heading to the front for a moment to hand the paper to Dallas, who glanced at it and nodded.

Chapter 52

Dallas read the email and then nodded. Thank you, Emma, this is the last link that I needed. I need to prove it, but you have done that. I thank God that we brought you in as a consultant. That helps a lot.

"Muir. Burnie. I am sorry once more that you had to go through what you did. Muir, you had no idea that you were to inherit that village, did you? Moira didn't either. A trust fund had been set up for you with the village as the trust, to come to you when you turned thirty. We have spoken with the lawyers who were involved. Your father didn't wish it to be a burden on you, he said. He would not have imagined what you went through in the last year or so.

"Burnie, when you walked into that store and stepped in, you had no idea what you were getting involved in. We have evidence, confirmed and all, that Holman was running an illegal gaming den or two in the village. The planes that you saw? They were ones that he had to bring in the gamblers. He refused to let them drive in, just knowing that too many cars would raise red flags. Stewart was not to have treated you as he did, Muir. You were to be held until you turned thirty or agreed to turn over the trust fund, which incidentally you cannot do. If you refuse it, it goes back to a trust for the village. No one will have access to it.

"Now as to your parents, Muir." He held up the email that he had just been handed. "Emma has come through once more. She has proof that your parents had been called back to Ireland on false pretences. The plan all along had been to kill them, but it had been planned to happen in Ireland. The authorities there have found a co-conspirator who has talked. The place went down in bad weather, from what we understand. It was a business class jet that had been sent over for your parents to travel on. You were to be with them, but your mother didn't want you to travel. That saved your life.

"Moira, Emma has more information for you that she will send on to you. Your property in Ireland was never sold but had been rented for years. The renters would like to purchase it, if you are willing. She has that contact information for you.

"Now, as to the Holman from here. He had been in Ireland, in contact with the business man that your father refused to deal with, Muir. He wanted revenge and Holman stepped in to help him. When your parents were killed, they went silent, until you were an adult. At that point, Stewart stepped in, wanting to destroy you to obtain control of the village. How he knew about the trust fund, he is not saying. We suspect that he searched your family's home at some point and found the paperwork. His plan all along had been to break you. His threats to send you out of the country were just that. Threats. Stewart had admitted that much in his statement before he was killed. He was involved in a lot of illegal activity.

"The person that you felt in the store building? You were correct. It was an associate of Stewart's, put there to make sure that you didn't escape. He was asleep when the fire hit and not likely even knew what had happened. We found his remains in the store debris in that ravine. We also found remains from six or seven other people. At this point, it is hard to determine if they were killed or died naturally and were buried. That is still being sorted out.

"You were correct when you stated that there was a room under the store, Muir. We have determined that it was used to hold supplies for the gambling dens. When the fire occurred, it was cleaned out. The shackles that you spotted in the photo? No has had yet explained them or their purpose. Any guess that we would or could make would just be speculation."

Dallas paused, his eyes roaming the room, fighting against a feeling of dread that he had. It was over for Muir, wasn't it? They had found everyone, had they not? He suddenly reached for a folder, opening it and then dropping it, before he was approaching Will.

The two men left quickly, heading for town and an abandoned building in the downtown area. They searched, patrol officers with them, finally pulling out an unkempt man, who maniacal gleam from his eye scared the officers. When questioned, he admitted that he had been hired to watch Muir and to let someone else know, someone that they had not expected.

Dallas had his phone out, calling Barnabas, letting him know that they had to finish up on another day. This left a lot of confusion in the building family, who finally moved away.

The next day, Dallas appeared in Burnie's office.

"Burnie, where's Muir?"

"In our apartment. Do you need to speak with her?"

"With both of you." Dallas followed Burnie through the apartment door, finding Muir standing staring at him.

"Dallas? You're back."

"I am. Sorry about yesterday. We had someone else to arrest, that I just discovered when I was speaking. Burnie, do you know that a post office employee was involved?"

Burnie went to shake his head and nodded instead. "Sean Foster."

"That's him. He was hired by Holman to watch you two, but he hired someone from the street. We have arrested both of them."

"It's over? It's finally over?" Muir turned to Burnie, swept into his arms in a hard hug.

"It is, Muir. It is. Thank goodness."

Epilogue

Two months later, Muir moved around the gardens, contentment rising within her. God had been good, she decided, and I am finally happy. I have searched all my life for this. God prepared it for me.

She had had a long talk with her Granny that day, finally. Moira had hugged her and then sat her down. She had told Muir of how difficult it had been those first few weeks and months after Moira had received the call from the authorities in Ireland that her parents' plane had disappeared from radar and they were unable to find it. They felt that the plane had disappeared into the Atlantic Ocean. Moira described how that day, her own face wet with tears, she had turned to pick the little one up from her nap, finding her inconsolable.

"You cried for hours for your Mommy, Muir." Moira's hand had rested on Muir head. "I couldn't calm you, couldn't console you. You would cry yourself to sleep and I would sit and just hold you, your little body shaking with sobs even as you slept. Then you would awaken and sob even harder. It was as if you knew that your mother was gone. This went on for days. I was grieving for Morgan and McRae and grieving for you as well. I had no minister that I could turn to. Only my old Bible and prayer."

"Did I know somehow, Granny?" Muir was thoughtful. She didn't remember her parents, they were only faces in faded photographs.

"I think that you did, Muir. You never asked for them as you grew, instead clinging tighter to me. I tried to explain it to you one day when you were about eight or so. You listened, asked no questions, and then just hugged me. I think that you were trying to comfort her."

"But God gave you comfort, didn't He? Does it say that?"

"He did, Muir. He did."

"Granny, I've thought about Michael. Was he an angel?"

"I don't know, Muir. He may have been. We'll not likely know until we reach Heaven and can ask."

The two ladies sat in silence, their arms around one another, before Muir began to tell Moira how she was now feeling and then hugged her Granny.

"Granny, I would not have made it had it not been for you. If you had still been in the village that day Burnie showed up, I wouldn't have left. I couldn't have left you there. Stewart would have tortured you."

"I know that he would have tried, Muir. But God provided in that, now didn't He?"

Muir turned as she heard footsteps and then ran for Burnie. He had been away that day, off on a book signing, and she had missed him. She had refused to go with him, saying that she just wanted to stay at home.

"Okay, sweetheart?" Burnie kissed her soundly.

"I am, now that you are home. How was the signing?" She grinned as he shrugged. "That bad?"

"No, it was okay. I just missed you. How was your day?"

"It was good. I spent some time with Granny, and then I finished proofreading that manuscript. I am enjoying that work, Burnie."

"I thought you would. Now, let's head into town. I want to take my sweetheart out for a meal."

"If you want. I would rather stay home." Muir grew pensive as they walked back towards the building. "Breck was around when I was in the gardens. He's heading off for a vacation, or so he says."

"He needs it. It's been a while since he had one." Burnie drew her down onto a bench near the entrance to the garden, listening to the sounds of nature, the late fall sun gleaming down on them. "I am glad that you are in my life, Muir."

"I am too." Muir frowned. "Michael?"

"What was that?" Burnie looked up, following the direction with his eyes that Muir was staring in.

"Michael was here. Oh, he's gone. Burnie, was he an angel?"

"I am sure that he was. God knew you needed that reminder." He hugged her tighter and just sat, content himself to be where he was. "I need to learn to trust Him more. This has been a learning experience for me."

"And for me. Thank you for teaching me, Burnie, in a way that I would understand." She looked up at him. "What now for the family here?"

Burnie shrugged. "Cadee and Benen and Devaney and Blair have had their babies. Brandon and Hagen's are growing. Baird and Berneen and Brennen and Jaxcy have announced that they are adding to their family." He grinned. "The parents that are here are over the moon, as they say. Granny is delighted, she says, to be great-granny to so many."

"She will be good at that. I don't know what I would have done without her." Muir's head went down against him. "Will we have little ones?"

"God only knows that, sweetheart. I pray that we do, but if we don't, we can always look at adopting."

"That's true. We can do that."

The couple grew quiet, their eyes on the setting sun, before they finally rose and walked, hand in hand, into the building.

Michael stood and watched before he looked up. "She's safe now, Lord. My work is finished. I will miss her, but I need to move on. Bless her and Burnie, Lord." Michael turned and walked away, disappearing into the rays of the setting sun.

Dear Readers

Thank you for choosing to read Burnie and Muir's story. He certainly threw in some added plot lines that I never saw coming. Must be the mystery writer in him.

Muir had been beaten down in many ways. As an orphan, she missed her parents and their guidance on her life greatly. Moira or Granny led her as best she could, teaching her to trust in God. That trust was sorely tried on many occasions.

I knew Burnie's would be one of those stories. He's a mystery writer and writers like to throw in plots and plans and curveballs. He is what I term as an unruly character, always ready to change the direction of the story. And he did that towards the end.

How do we teach someone to trust in God, to depend on Him? First, by our example. Then, by directing them back to His word. Our Christian walk should be that: teaching others, leading them to a closer walk with Him. We are human, and we stumble and fall and fail. But we pick ourselves up, dust ourselves off and continue on, our hand in Him.

Of course, Abe and Emma and his men and ladies had to show up again. Their stories are in try *His Guardians* series. Beloved characters that just have to keep coming back. Doug and Darcie's story is in *The Heart of a Lion*, written as a challenge for my first Nanowrimo try.

Now, Michael? Was he an angel or wasn't he? I leave that up to you to decide. I firmly believe that there are occasions when angels become visible presences to help us.

God bless.

Ronna

Lightning Source UK Ltd.
Milton Keynes UK
UKHW020636011220
374435UK00012B/1106